How To Marry A Marble Marquis

A Regency Monster Romance

C.M. Nascosta

MEDUAS
EDITORIALE

Dedication

This is where I'm supposed to write some pithy little Instagrammable sound bite, but this book isn't dedicated to anyone but me. Keep up the great work, gorgeous!

The High Tea

SOCIETY PAPERS

Dearest Readers,

Welcome to the High Tea, where the ton's every misstep is served up with a piping fresh pot of scandal.

In this book, you will find plucky heroines, unrepentant rakes who act like rakes (that means relationships outside of his with our FMC, dear readers) discussions of poverty and peerage, knotting and sleep play, mentions of self-harm of the stone variety, and more saucy banter than we can hold in a pot.

This is a standalone Regency Monster Romance that takes place within the shared world of the Monsters Ball, but it is also the beginning of the much anticipated Talons & Temptations series from your author – please see her back matter to learn more on what's coming next!

Until next time, sip slowly, my dears.

Lady Grey

The High Tea

SOCIETY PAPERS

Sweet sippers, do we have a scandal for you!

Some attendees of Lady Harthington's resplendent Snowdrop Ball received an eye full of more than they'd likely expected to see this past week. Cuckolded by his own valet in plain sight of the manor — a parvenue scandal with a capital P! Our loyal little serving spoons tell us the lady of disrepute was one Miss E, and we have no doubt the wick she had left on the embers of his Lordship's generosity has been thoroughly extinguished. This tea trollop has surely seen the end on her season, for no respectable lady would act in such a way. Good riddance, we say!

Sip slowly, my dears!

Lady Grey

Eleanor

Dear Miss Eastwick,

On account of the unfortunate incident involving Lord Pemberly and his valet at Lady Harthington's Ball, Her Majesty has no choice but to deem your Season a failure. With no other suitors of an appropriate station and no dowry, you are hereby ordered to attend the Monsters Ball, your last hope of securing a marriage for the Season.

The parchment crumpled in her fist as her hand closed. The letter from the Queen was the ultimate humiliation. *So kind of Her Majesty to ensure you'll never forget how utterly inept and unmarriageable you are.* Eleanor wasn't sure why she kept punishing herself by reading it over and over again. Perhaps as a way to remind herself of the precariousness of her position and how important this last card to play was, she reminded herself, placing the letter in an empty drawer, tucked out of sight, wishing she could hide away her humiliation as easily.

The High Tea had recounted the entire mortifying incident to all of London society, making her and Lord Pemberley both laughingstocks. *Some attendees of Lady Harthington's resplendent Snowdrop Ball received an eye full of more than they'd likely expected to see this past week. Cuckolded by his own valet in plain sight of the manor — a parvenue scandal with a capital* **P***! Our loyal little serving spoons tell us the lady of disrepute was one* **Miss E***, and we have no doubt the* **wick** *she had left on the* **embers** *of his Lordship's generosity has been thoroughly extinguished. Good riddance, we say!*

Her face heated further at the thought. The High Tea was the scourge of London. A gossip publication devoted to the ton's marriage market, they had eyes at every ball, every garden soirée, every riding excursion, and game of croquet. *Perhaps he hadn't seen it.* After all, lords of high standing had no use for trivial gossip. This

Marquis of Basingstone likely wouldn't either. *I'm sure he has more important things to worry about than some silly inaccurate slander.*

The incident with Lord Pemberley's valet was not her fault. The man was rude and quite insistent in his failed manners, and she hadn't required his assistance in the first place. If he was going to offer his hand to help her descend the carriage steps, the least he could have done was to ensure the pathway was cleared of loose stones and frolicking spaniels. That Lord Pemberley had turned just in time to see her sprawled out over his manservant — her knees coming down on either side of his legs as if she were mounting a horse, clawing at his waistcoat to regain her balance, the man's big hand attempting to steady her and instead cupping a generous handful of her posterior — was all simply a dreadful misunderstanding.

She should have cut her losses then, but like the foolish optimist she was, she had continued into the ball, hoping against hope that the incident outside would remain in the dust. Her faith in her fellow revelers was misplaced. Lady Harthington eyed her as if she were a particularly unattractive bug every time Eleanor happened to find herself in the crosshairs of the woman's gaze, and Lord Pemberley seemed intent on forgetting she existed. She wound up spending most of the evening sitting at a cluster of tables with the other wallflowers, wishing she had simply stayed in Paris.

A failure. A failure. A failure. Heat rose to her cheeks every time she read the blasted missive, and Eleanor knew that moment was no exception. *Pull yourself together. He's going to be here any moment; you don't need to look like a strawberry when he does.*

Resting her forehead against the cool marble on the side of the fireplace, she sucked in a centering breath, counting to three before turning, casting her gaze over the room once more. Everything was perfect. Or at least as perfect as they could make it under the circumstances. The table was set for tea. The sterling tea service belonged to her grandmother, a wedding gift, and Eleanor had repolished it that morning herself, ensuring that she could see her face in the surface of the pot and sugar bowl and in each dainty spoon. Fresh flowers were set in a cut crystal vase in the center of the table, and the firelight winked off the leaded glass. If the sun were shining, it would have cast her prison of rainbows on the far wall beyond the base, but as it was the middle of the night, the effect was only aided by the lamps and candles around the room.

Eleanor went around fluffing chintz pillows and straightening the curtains, ensuring the side window that overlooked the garden was framed in a way that gave the room an ethereal, moonlit glow. Lucy had been practicing her tea-making skills for nearly two weeks in preparation for that night. She'd finally achieved the mastery of steeping the tea just long enough to achieve a rich golden hue from the tightly rolled leaves, removing the kettle from the heat and decanting the leaf-less tea into the sterling pot before it turned bitter. She and Coraline had painstakingly prepared the dainty savories, turning each tiny square of quiche and smoked ham into a culinary delicacy fit for the Queen herself. *Hopefully, fit enough for the Marquis of Basingstone.* His Lordship didn't need to know that his meal had been prepared by children, for she certainly didn't anticipate that he would ask to speak with the cook.

The tea service would fetch a fine price at auction if it came to that. The tea set and the needlepoint chairs, the fine crystal, and all of the porcelain. The grandfather clock in the front hall had a face inlaid with moth-er-of-pearl, and Eleanor was certain that, too, would do handsomely if it was sold to the right bidder. She had already sold off most of mother's jewelry, saving one special piece for each of the girls. Father's silver-topped walking stick had gone the way of the baubles and gems, along with the pianoforte that had been her en-tire childhood. Soon the house would be an empty shell as she sold off their belongings one by one. Like a cav-ernous dollhouse, devoid of furniture or dolls or any carefree little girl to play with it, all of their memories and fine things scattered to the wind like ashes.

Stop it. He's going to be here any moment. You need to remember yourself. Remember your manners. Show him that you are, in fact, a lady of good standing. Uncle Efraim wouldn't have suggested this if the Monsters Ball wasn't your last hope. Drawing in another deep breath, Eleanor moved back to the fireplace, posing herself in a way that she hoped was alluring, and readied herself. She was already able to hear the clip-clop of horse hooves and knew that would likely be his carriage. *This is it.* She was going to be taking courting advice from some dreadful old man, possibly one with a wandering hand, but if he had a nephew or a cousin of marrying age, it would be all worth it in the end. *You're doing this for the girl.*

Her head felt heavy as he was announced, her grandmother's nurse doing a valiant job at playing house servant for the night. Hettie was attempting to disguise her country accent with what she probably thought was meant to be posh, but wound up sounding as if she'd only learned the common tongue that same day.

"The Marquis of Basingstone has come to call, Miss."

Hettie stepped aside, the gargoyle behind her moving forward, his nose in the air, and Eleanor froze. She didn't know why she had been picturing someone of an age with uncle Efraim. Perhaps it was the stuffiness of his title or the fact that he knew uncle Efraim at all. She had envisioned a gentleman even older than the earl — white of hair and wrinkled of face, perhaps with a cane. She had been berating herself for this mad plan all week, not understanding the earl's suggestion, nor why taking advice from some old man would do her any good in finding a husband, but now — now she understood perfectly.

The Marquis of Basingstone was far younger than she had anticipated. Perhaps a decade older than herself, at most. He *did* have white hair, she sniffed. A shock of silver-white hair tumbling appealingly over a sharply arched brow of the same snowy color. Twisting horns sprouted from his head, pushing through his white hair like the twinned spires of mountains above a lush valley of snow. His skin was black as pitch, veined in the same luminous white of his hair, almost glowing across cheekbones so sharp, she wondered if he'd ever accidentally cut himself. He was devilishly handsome, and to add insult to injury, his figure was as appealing as his face. The intricate jacquard on his waistcoat stretched across a broad, well-muscled chest that tapered to a waspish waist, and the cherry-sized sapphire pinned at the center of his cravat was the same shade of blue as his narrowed eyes. His trousers looked practically painted on, disappearing into high Hessian boots, the shine upon which rivaled her tea setting.

Eleanor consoled herself that while she was gaping at him as if she'd never seen a member of the opposite sex before, he was taking her in just as thoroughly. She felt the drag of those keen blue eyes up her form and wondered if he could tell that her dress was twice turned already. As he took a step further into the room, his wide wings blotted out the sight of the housekeeper altogether, and his tight-lipped smile curved, arriving at her eyes at last.

"Lord Stride," she finally squeaked out, remembering herself. "I'm so grateful you were able to come this evening. Thank you, Hettie. That will be all for now, but you can begin preparing our tea."

"Miss Eastwick," the gargoyle before her purred, taking her proffered hand as soon as the door had clicked shut behind them. "Thank you for your most gracious invitation."

If Hettie had wished to sound posh for the evening, conversing several minutes with Lord Silas Stride would have served as an ample lesson in the elocution of the nobility. His voice was silky, practically a drawl, managing to sound lofty and bored out of his mind simultaneously. He enunciated every crisp consonant and hung on each voluptuous vowel, his voice icy and white, like a slide of satin, as striking as his appearance.

"I admit," he sniffed, his gloved hand releasing hers at last, "to being quite intrigued by the correspondence I received from the Earl of Chwyllenghd."

"I'm so grateful to him for writing to you. Please, let's sit." Eleanor held her breath as the Marquis came around the table, pulling her chair out with a little bow. He was cordial enough, but he was so *un*like what she was expecting — a doddering old man with a wild shock of hair coming from his ears, perhaps — that she felt completely unprepared for the rest of the night. All of her careful preparations and rehearsed speeches had been designed for someone old enough to be her grandfather, who might look at her with the kindly eyes of the village vicar, or else, some lecherous old uncle who would gape at her décolleté, make ribald jokes, and each facet of her plan seemed woefully ill-prepared now. When he was last seated across from her, she finally dared to blink.

"It's a very fair evening," she chirped, hoping she sounded serene and unflappable and not at all like someone who was content to roll around with a footman in plain sight of the household. "I'm quite relieved the weather has remained so mild. This time of year can sometimes be so unpredictable."

He eyed her with an inscrutable look for an endless heartbeat before a lopsided smile split his features, giving her a hint of gleaming white fang. "It is indeed a fair evening. You chose a fortuitous night for our little liaison."

"Yes," she laughed nervously. "I confess, my Lord, I'm not actually certain how far it was you had to travel. Unc — Lord Ellingboe did not mention how far your residence is. I do hope it wasn't too arduous a journey."

The penetrating look had not yet eased up, and Eleanor squirmed under the weight of his cool blue eyes. It seemed to her as if he were waiting for her to make some horrid blunder, and she wondered if the story of Lady Harthington's ball had already reached his long, pointed ears. She could already hear the tea cart making its way down the hall, and could imagine Lucy and Coraline both skipping along beside it, ensuring their miniature culinary masterpieces were perfectly placed.

"Not at all, Miss Eastwick. I was already in London, as it were. I'll be returning to Basingstone this week to settle some affairs and then relocating to London for the next few months. Londonderry is so dreadfully dull this time of year; I'll be glad for the change of scenery."

She gave him her most charming smile. "I'm sure your duties keep you busy, my Lord. Although that coastal scenery is likely quite restorative for one's health, even if the town is dreadfully dull."

Another tight-lipped grin, his eyes still searching. "As restorative as rain-soaked cliffs have the power of being, I suppose. And how is it that you are acquainted with the earl, Miss Eastwick?"

"Oh, of-of course. Well, you see, Lord Ellingboe was a friend of my father. They became acquainted when my father was staying up in the northern country before he'd even met my mother. They were both fond of—"

"I'm more curious," he interrupted, one of his white brows arching sardonically, "as to why exactly the Earl of Chwyllenghd is so interested in the marriage prospects of a woman who is neither his daughter nor his mistress, nor even his ward? I would expect such consternation over a daughter with three seasons behind her, even coming from a concerned aunt or grandmother. It seems unusual for the same concern to originate from a wholly uninvested party, you see."

Eleanor felt each word like a blow, each more humiliating than the last. He must have interpreted her stricken look correctly, for he shrugged gracefully, shaking his hair from his brow with a toss of his head. A shrug was hardly conciliatory, she thought furiously, for he'd essentially called her a spinster with no prospects, and a suspicious one at that.

"Come now, Miss Eastwick. We've discussed the weather and the restorative properties of the northern cliffs. As enchanting as your company might be, I'm certain exchanging the most banal of pleasantries is not why I was written to join you for tea."

The tea cart had arrived, saving her from her shock over his shocking and frankly *inexcusable* rudeness. Eleanor had known men like him, lords like him, and they were all the same — utter prats. She would have been happy to cut the marquis's visit short, but from her position facing the door, she was able to see the two small heads attempting to peer invisibly around the jamb as Hettie pushed the rattling cart into the room, reminding her that she wasn't doing this for herself. The conversation paused as the aged nurse carefully placed the three-tiered tray on the center of the table, along with the gleaming silver pot.

Eleanor watched the Marquis of Basingstone taking advantage of the distraction to cast his sharp blue gaze around the room. She wondered what he saw, if he could tell where the piano had once stood, or if could see the slight discoloration of the wood on the shelves that had once been full of books. When Hettie took her leave once more, he turned to face her again, resuming the conversation as if there had been no interruption at all.

"The letter I received from the earl was woefully thin on what, specifically, was being requested of me. I crave your indulgence, Miss Eastwick. I've always been dreadful at waiting for things. Patience is, regrettably, one of the many virtues I lack."

Eleanor folded her hands in her lap primly. She was in danger of biting her tongue hard enough to draw blood as she pressed her lips together tightly in a smile, wondering if he could see the daggers in her eyes. *What a rude man. They're all the same, these lords. Only good for one thing — the security they can provide.* If only Lord Ellingboe was still in London, her situation might not be as dire. Alas, the earl had retired to his manor house, his eldest son and heir moving into the London residence and assuming the duties of the title. She'd only met the stony son of the orc lord once, but it had been enough for her to understand he'd not be as willing to take on a charity case as his father.

Uncle Efraim had done enough by writing to this marquis. *And now you can't go squandering the opportunity; you can't afford to. Think of the girls.* This gargoyle was the same sort of fop who would crowd around the backstage area at the theater, attempting to press roses into her arms and take her to dinner, a surefire way, they always thought, of getting under her skirts. She had never needed any of them then, and she'd never given in to their artificial charms. *And we won't be giving into this one either, but we **do** need his connections.*

She cleared her throat, wondering if there was any sense in trying to dance around the truth. *Not likely. Just get on with it.* "Uncle Efraim was a good friend of my late father," she began again, a thread of ice accompanying her words. "My parents are gone. A carriage accident. I was . . . staying abroad at the time, but after the accident I returned to London to be a guardian to my younger sisters. You're quite right, Lord Stride, I am hardly of an age to be entering society for the first time. I would prefer to focus on securing a future match for my sister, but—"

"But you need to marry yourself to have the ability to do so," he interrupted again, reaching the conclusion of her story before she could do so herself.

"We don't have any close family," she went on through gritted teeth. "Lord Ellingboe heard about my recent . . . misfortunes and—"

"Ah yes, the *parvenue scandal with a capital P*."

Eleanor wondered if she would ever be able to complete a sentence while in the Marquis of Basingstone's haughty company. He chuckled, and that, too, was an icy white sound.

"It's as if they don't even make an attempt to be clever sometimes. As someone whose exploits have been regularly and thoroughly excoriated by the High Tea, if it is any consolation, my dear Miss Eastwick, you can rest assured that by the next edition, no one remembers anything from the previous week. There's always a new target."

She was going to need to have the inside of her lip sewn up once this evening was through, Eleanor thought as she practically chewed a hole into it, a desperate effort to keep her occasionally barbed tongue from finding its target in the gargoyle across from her.

"You do have my deepest sympathies for your loss," he went on, his voice losing a fraction of its chill. "I, too, have experienced the unfortunate role of being orphaned in adulthood with younger siblings to think of. I take it that Lord Ellingboe was the one to sponsor your season then?" he continued. "Although, I am a bit surprised that he went to such lengths on your behalf rather than simply finding a match for you himself here in London. I suppose that owes to the fact that the earl has vacated London completely. A premature decision, in my opinion, but that's Northerners for you."

She exhaled slowly through her nose, determined to keep her voice light. "Begging your pardon, Lord Stride, but is Londonderry not in the north? I hadn't realized those rain-soaked cliffs had been relocated."

His mouth split, another flash of white fang, although his smile reached his eyes this time, sparkling across the table, as blue and shining as the sapphire he wore, and her breath caught in spite of herself. "So it is, Miss Eastwick. So it is. Now just to ensure I'm keeping the details straight, Lord Ellingboe sponsored your season.

A season that I'm assuming is now over, thanks to Lord Pemberley's valet, more's the pity, my dear."

"Not over quite yet, my lord," she bit out, ignoring his jab. "I shall be attending the Monster's Ball. Uncle Efraim sponsored my season for the same reason he wrote to you on my behalf."

She hesitated, watching his eyebrow raise in expectation. She felt as if she were standing in the center of the stage, a limelight casting her in a halo, holding her breath before the music began. That was always the most fraught moment, the most vulnerable. Just her alone, standing before a sea of onlookers she couldn't make out. She was just as alone now. Heat crept up her neck, and Eleanor had the terrible feeling she was near tears. Her eyes fought away from his, disliking their cold appraisal . . . but all around her were the reminders of why this meeting was so important. The empty shelves where a library of books had once stood, books she'd sold one by one, the missing furniture. Her sisters would wind up as seamstresses and governesses, never enjoying a home of their own at this rate. *You don't have a choice.*

"I-I don't know what I'm doing, Lord Stride. Obviously. I have proven to be," she sighed forcefully, "a bit of a hopeless case. Lord Ellingboe thought you would be admirably positioned to instruct me to increase my chances of success."

"Instruct you?"

"On how to win a husband at the Monster's Ball. I've not had fair fortune with men of my own species, let alone navigating the social waters within a community in which I am completely inexperienced. I am not able to pay you to do so, but I'm committed to making up for the use of your time in any way you deem necessary. I am hoping you will be amenable to the request, but I understand, my Lord, if you find it too peculiar."

Silence stretched between them, the marquis still appraising at her as if he were waiting for her to burst into flames. Eleanor felt her heart sink like a stone within her. *This was all a waste of time. You may as well pack up the girls now and try to find employment in some lord's country house. If you're lucky, you can all stay together.*

"Traveling abroad, you mentioned . . . most unusual. Do you often take tea in the middle of the night, Miss Eastwick?"

His question was unexpected and his tone overly casual. Eleanor floundered. She was grateful for the break in the topic, for it allowed her to suck in a breath and push back the tears that had been hovering just beneath the surface of her composure, but the question itself left her feeling unmoored. "I-I beg your pardon, my lord?"

He gestured to the full afternoon tea service before them before lifting his cup, taking a long swallow before resuming. "Do you often enjoy afternoon tea at nearly two a.m., Miss Eastwick?"

Eleanor snapped her mouth shut after a moment, realizing she had opened it in shock at the audacity of such a question. *Of course not, and he bloody well knows it.* "I don't, my lord, no. Although, I *am* often up at this hour. Sleep does not find me easily these days, and I've always been a bit of a night owl. I've never entertained company of the nocturnal persuasion, and I only sought to make your visit more comfortable, Lord Stride. My sincerest apologies if we failed in our attempt."

The Marquis of Basingstone grinned, chuckling to himself. *Perhaps he'll hurry up and leave once he says no. The less you have to look upon his smug smirk, the better, and you'll never need to see him again.*

"You intimate that you lack social graces and you've no experience with the monstrous gentry, and yet," he drawled, draining his cup, "you took into account the time of our little tête-à-tête, understood that this would be what you would consider the middle of the after-noon for me, and you made accommodations to the best of your ability. You are a charming hostess, a genial con-versationalist, I'm assuming, when you don't have such a rude partner, of course, and lovely to behold, if not a bit conservative. I don't find you hopeless at all, Miss Eastwick. I accept your offer. I should be glad to help you secure a husband at the Monsters Ball. As a matter of fact, I can guarantee it. The joy of your company will be payment enough, of that, I have little doubt. My only request is that you do exactly as I say and don't second guess my methodology. By the time I'm through with you, you will have your choice of suitors."

He left shortly thereafter, and by the time his carriage disappeared into the dark road, Eleanor was slumped against the door. The tiered tray of sweets and savories had barely been touched, but it was expensive meat and cheese, too fine to go to waste, and the girls would enjoy the tiny delicacies the following day.

He was going to help her, she reminded herself, finally trudging to bed, only an hour or two before dawn. He was going to help her and things were going to work out. It didn't matter that she would be marrying a stranger, both in personality and form, nor did it matter that the Marquis of Basingstone and his sharp gaze left her discomfited. She was simply going to have to get used to it. *You're going to be spending a lot of time in his company over the next few weeks. What was that he said? He would be in London indefinitely for the next several months? Plenty of time to flourish under his tutelage.* Optimistic words. Aspirational, even. Something to strive for, to do right for a change.

At least, Eleanor thought, closing her eyes determinedly, he was nice to look at. *If nothing else, he's handsome. Who cares if he's rude. He's a lord, of course he's a snob, what did you expect? He's also the one who's going to get you out of this mess.* She knew that, knew that he was her only hope, but that didn't keep her stomach from braiding itself into knots at the thought of spending any more time in his cool, condescending company.

Silas

The manor at Basingstone was an oasis of sun-bleached stone walls, climbing with ivy and winking with more than a hundred palladium windows, the leaded glass gleaming in the sunlight each afternoon. The prize-winning rose garden was a resplendent sea of color, the petals kissed with dew in the early dawn hours, and the topiaries that lined the long gravel pathway cast jumping shapes across the lawn in the high, midday sun. There was a breeding pair of mute swans that nested on the grounds, he was told, and every spring, they would glide regally across the lake, downy little cygnets paddling furiously behind them in the golden, sun-kissed afternoons. The rolling hills behind them were lush and green, and the majestic cliffs before them overlooked the ever-crashing waves. Basingstone was lovely in the day. Or, at least, so he'd been told.

Silas had never been awake to appreciate the sight of his ancestral home in the morning hours, nor had he ever experienced a stroll through the rose garden when the petals still held the glimmer of dew. He could not tell what sort of rainbow display the winking leaded glass of the windows was meant to create, having never seen it for himself, and whatever shadows the sun cast on the topiaries in the afternoon, it surely paled to what the moon did after midnight, he was certain — her icy white light creating longer, leering shapes that leapt across the gravel. He had never seen the swans swimming in the midday sun and wasn't sure if he'd know a cygnet if he stepped on one. He had no idea what his home looked like in the hours before dusk, and he was sick to death of hearing about it thirdhand from near strangers.

"He said that a decision must be made soon, my lord, before the weather changes too thoroughly. If you'd like, I can consult with the house steward at Killendare and ask what course of action they've—"

"Just do whatever it is you need to do, for the love of the moon, Kestin," he interrupted his steward, stopping the mothman's long-winded soliloquy on whatever it was the groundskeeper had relayed needed to be done before the spring season fully returned. Silas felt a tension headache brewing behind his eye, a half dozen members of the household vying for his attention all bloody evening, a consequence of his time in London but still an absolute nuisance, and all he wanted was to be left alone to nurse his brandy and brood in peace. "I don't bloody care. Prune back the roses, set them on fire; it makes no difference to me. Just do it without needing me to hear about it."

Kestin had been at Basingtone for nearly two decades, a comfort in his position that was evidenced by the way the mothman's lip curled back, his nose rising a fraction as his wings rustled in offense. Silas rolled his eyes. He had returned to Basingstone the previous night, and evidently his steward-in-residence had expected to be cosseted like a child who'd been left alone for the summer holiday. Silas turned away, refusing to be cowed by the feathery antennae that had straightened out like arrows.

"Is there anything else?"

"Yes, my lord." The mothman gave him a patronizing smile. "Your sister is here."

Silas's head dropped, shoulders slumping as he waved Kestin away. He wasn't sure *why* he'd expected a single night's peace, a preposterously foolish notion, he understood now, for the study door had scarcely closed behind the steward before Silas heard her voice.

"Silas!"

He wasn't certain what his sister Maris ever meant to achieve by shouting his name from down the hall. He had no intention of leaving his study, and she still had an entire corridor to traverse, yet this was how she opted to announce her presence every time she came to visit him, which was every time he was in residence at the manor. That ridiculousness of shouting had never stopped Maris before, and that evening would be no different, apparently.

"Silas!"

"Maris, darling, please don't shout," he called through the closed door, his voice flat, uncaring if she heard him or not. "You can raise your voice all you want. It doesn't mean I'm getting up for you."

His sister burst into the study, not bothering to knock. It had always been this way. There were four years that separated them, but Maris had decided sometime around the age of seven or eight that she no longer needed to take his orders, despite the fact that *he* was the one with the title.

"Why didn't you tell me you were coming home?" she asked peevishly, flouncing to the chair before to his desk, seating herself without invitation. "You could have sent word, you know. I would've had a welcoming dinner prepared for you."

"Unnecessary," he muttered. "In any case, I won't be here long."

"You're never here long," she shot back. "Just long enough to cause trouble before you flit back to London and leave us to pick up the pieces."

"Well, I daresay I won't be here long enough to cause any trouble, love," he lied smoothly. He had every intention of paying a visit to the fair lady of Derrybrook that night, having run into her husband the previous evening as the lord journeyed to London. Draining his balls before going to bed was a sure way to ensure his headache would be extinguished while he slept, and Lady Derrybrook had a fantastically firm grip.

Maris rolled her eyes, clearly not believing him. "We really need to throw a ball, you know. Invite all of the most eligible—"

"No."

"But Silas, we need to start finding you a—"

"Maris, I said no."

"Well, are you at least staying long enough so that we can invite the Countess of —"

"*Maris.*"

Her mouth snapped shut at last, glaring at him.

"I'm not," he went on succinctly. "I need to be getting back to London before the end of the week, actually. I've only come back to deal with the accounts and to make sure that you're set up with everything you require for the season, darling. And besides, I don't think I would be very welcome at any table across from the Countess of Crevingsham unless she's acquired a concussion and no longer remembers the incident involving her sister."

Across the desk, his sister grumbled. He couldn't quite make out her words, but he was certain he managed to catch *appalling behavior* quickly followed by *thinking with your cock* before her mouth set in a firm line, resembling their mother so entirely that he nearly shuddered.

He and Maris had been told they resembled twins since they were children, and he knew the sour look she was directing at him was likely identical to the one he had given Kestin only minutes earlier. Her silver-white hair was twisted into a thick plait that began at her temples, the long length of it winding back up to curl around her head like a crown. The white veining shot through her jet skin was dusted in a powder that gave it a luminous glow, and her lips were painted to look like plump cherries. The only marked difference in their outward appearance was her slightness, her wings more angular, taking on the guise of a bird rather than a bat. She'd had her horns capped in silver the previous winter, and Silas was forced to admit that the effect — her crown-like hair, the winking silver, her haughty expression – coalesced into something more lord-like than he probably managed on a day-to-day basis. *All the better. Proof that your plan is a good one.*

"I'll be reviewing the accounts tomorrow evening," he pushed on, changing the subject to things that actually mattered. "You have unlimited access and absolute authority in my absence, you know that. Don't let me come back here to find little Silas sleeping in a cradle *not* adorned with moonstones and silver, so you understand?"

She laughed, her hands landing on the swell of her stomach almost without her conscious choice. She was looking well, he thought. Silas knew she was worried. Their mother had died in childbirth, the egg she'd been carrying never hatching, a double loss from which their father never recovered. He'd not been lying to Eleanor Eastwick when he'd offered his condolences, knowing exactly the burden that rested on her attractive shoulders. His sister was well-positioned to carry on the family line, and if at least one of her children were named after him, he would be satisfied.

"I think it's a girl. I don't know why, it's just a feeling I have . . . Have you heard from Cadmus?" Her voice softened, and Silas nodded, indicating the unopened parchment on the desk before him.

"I have, although I've not read it yet. I think it's safe to assume he's not dead if we're still receiving things."

Maris huffed. "Don't even joke about something like that! How dreadful. He sent me the loveliest dress. It's bright blue, like a peacock, and hand-painted. The embroidery around the neckline has little shells in it – shells! The tiniest little things, right from the sea! It's so beautiful. I've no idea where I'll have a chance to wear it, or even if it will fit me right now, and it's so exotic, but I love it. I do miss him so, Silas. Can't you write to him? Ask him to come home?"

"This isn't his home, Maris. It never was. It wasn't his life. Mother made certain he knew that. He has his own life out there, somewhere."

His sister lowered her eyes, and the silence that hung between them held the extra weight of their absent eldest sibling.

"We need to plan a ball," she began after a moment in a slow, measured voice, quickly raising a placating hand. "Not for this week, obviously. Sometime this spring. Pick a week when you're not needed in London, preferably after the rainy season, and I can begin planning it. We need to find you a wife, Silas. It's far past time that you wed."

"It sounds like you're attempting to trot me out like some prize-winning spaniel. Does a collar come with this ball of yours?"

"The Monsters Ball is coming up, is it not?" she sniffed after a long moment of glaring at him. "I do hope you are prepared? At this point, I don't even care who you marry, only that you do. It's bad enough that you brokered my marriage like some bloody banker, but now you expect me to be *your* broodmare. It's horribly unfair, Silas."

"It's almost as if you're not enjoying married life, dear. Someone should let Luenn know."

"You can go right ahead and do that," she shot back, "because we all know he's your chosen puppet. I don't know what game you're playing at Silas, but you're not a child anymore. It's time to do your part. *You* have a duty to the family name."

Silas opened his mouth to speak, but his sister didn't give him a chance, plowing on, barely taking a breath.

"You sent me out for my season, and I married the man you hand-picked for me without complaint because I knew that was *my* role. My duty to the family. Now I'm carrying a child who'll end up as your ward because you don't have an heir. And again, that's my duty. If you don't come home from the Monster's Ball with a fiancée, then I'm planning a ball upon your return, and you *will* marry someone. Perhaps of *my* choosing, just to even things off a bit. I don't even care if she can bear your child. I'll be sure to give you another with your bloody name. I've done my duty, Silas. It's time to stop faffing about and do yours."

By the time Maris left, his head was throbbing. The most annoying bit was that he knew she was right. He was doing a horrible job at carrying out his duty to the family name, and he was being terribly unfair to his sister. It *only feels unfair right now. When she's wearing the title, it will all make sense.* Slicing open the letter from his brother, Silas pushed away thoughts of his sister's plan for him. His plan for her was far more prescient, after all.

Little brother,

I'm writing to you from the balcony of a pleasure house, one of great repute, where I have spent far too much coin in the past several days. Days in which I've only been ver-

tical for short bursts at a time, just long enough to eat and replenish my energy. There is a courtesier here for every act and appetite, no matter how deviant. The young lady whose company I enjoyed this morning boasted that after suffering from a choking accident when she was just a girl, she had no gag reflex to speak of. I took her bet, and I'm quite delighted to report that she did not, in fact, have a gag reflex.

Below the window, as I'm writing, there is a fight taking place in the street. One man has a pistol, while the other is in possession of the sort of sword that can take a man's arm off before he has the time to pull his trigger. I'm quite certain the fellow with the pistol is unaware of this fact, but he's likely about to learn in the most unfortunate manner.

All of which is a very long way of telling you that you would love it here. Bear in mind, I still think your plan is utter madness and that you need to come to your senses. I shudder to think of how much weight you would shed and coin you would spend in a port like this. We'll find you at the end of the first month in some back alley, emaciated and dehydrated, your purse empty and your cock reduced to pulp, so perhaps it is a relief that you are on the other side of the world.

We're going to be traveling off-realm soon. I know that means little to you, for the magic contained at sea is not something one would ever encounter in Londonderry. Captains of the star sea are less predictable than those who journey by water, and it's always a delicate dance, mixing with them and not causing inadvertent offense. Suffice it to say it is dangerous, and I hope to be back in our own realm relatively quickly.

I expect to find correspondence from you at our next port of call, Perico, where you've left letters before. In the event that there is not, I shall simply have to find a better recipient for the package I intended on sending ahead. I'll be sending a parcel for Maris from there, with the Basingstone address. Please see that it finds its way to her.

It's not too late to set a better course for your life, Silas. The only obstacle you've ever had is your own bloody head. Put away these foolish plans of yours and start looking to the future of your legacy in a manner that doesn't include bedding the wife of every other lord in the countryside.

And just as a reminder — you can't even fucking swim.

In the event I do not return, all of my worldly possessions, most of which can be found on Dragonfly Island, are be-

queathed to you, Lord Silas Stride, Marquis of Basingstone. Please do split the plunder with Maris accordingly.

Yours most affectionately,

Cadmus

Silas let out a hard breath. He wondered how Maris would fare being the recipient of Cadmus's last will and testament as a signoff in every correspondence their brother sent. *She'll get used to it eventually*.

The parcel that accompanied the letter contained a goblet carved from shell, the intricately designed seascape on its side breathtaking to behold. Within the goblet was a sack of coins. Silas tugged the cord, tipping the sack, letting them spill out on the desk. They were larger than the common gold Griffin in circulation, and upon his examination, he discovered they were brothel tokens, each one showing a number on one side, evidently the denomination, and a topless mermaid on the other, her voluptuous curves nearly overshadowed by the brightness of her smile. Laughing, he wondered if he would have the chance to make good use of these eventually.

Closing his eyes, he tipped his head back for a long moment, willing the pain in his head away before opening the top drawer of the desk, retrieving his quill and a clean sheet of foolscap. Dipping the nib into the pot of ink on the leather desk cover, he began to write.

Dearest brother,

Despite your wretched instance in closing each letter in a way that makes it sound as if you're planning on putting your cock in the mouth of the nearest shark, I'm always relieved to receive correspondence from you. I wonder if the regular updates to your will are meant to make you feel better, or if you're trying to entice me to Dragonfly Island to plunder your possessions in your absence.

There is indeed a letter waiting for you at Port Perico, you'll be pleased to know. I believe, at the time of its posting, I had recently spent the day on a foreign rooftop after a rather infelicitous greeting by the Duke of Shoretham. The hospitality of his house was lacking, regrettably, but I had no such complaints over the hospitality of his wife.

Your assumption that I would find the conditions you outlined in your letter enjoyable is correct. I do hope the young woman wasn't unduly injured in her accident, but the loss of the gag reflex is a seldom-found attribute in London, and I am wickedly jealous of your luck.

I have returned to Basingstone for the week to settle some accounts and ensure Maris has everything she needs to be comfortable. Her pregnancy is progressing without issue, and she seems to be in good spirits, aside from haranguing me the instant my feet cross the threshold of the house. She has asked me, as she always does, to demand you to return home, but I don't think she's considering the state of her wardrobe if I were to do so.

It will come as no surprise to you that she is quite intent on finding me a wife. The Monster's Ball is the final festivity on the calendar for the season, and she has already given me the ultimatum that I return home from that soirée affianced or else she will take matters into her own hands, finding me a wife as I found Luenn for her.

Since you have no issue signing off your correspondence with me in the most morbid way possible, I shall remind you of what I sent in my last letter — I have no intentions of marrying. My plan may seem foolhardy to you, but you have been at sea for far too long, and I read that ingesting sea water can turn a man's mind. I beg you, bother — stop drinking the sea water. And what need have I for swimming? Isn't that the whole bloody point of the ship?

*I <u>will</u> be paying close attention to the Monster's Ball this year, only not for the reason Maris hopes. I received correspondence from Efraim Ellingboe seeking my assistance in finding a husband for a young woman he has sponsored. You were such close friends with his eldest son, I felt compelled to meet with the girl, just to see what it was all about. I recognized her the instant I stepped into the room, although I am still unable to place from where. It has been itching at my mind for the past three days. I suppose this is the result of saying hello with my cock first for so many years, but I **know** that I know her somehow.*

As it is, I have agreed to offer the girl tutelage in the fairer arts of seduction so that she may find herself a husband at the Monster's Ball. I would not normally offer the gift of my time in such a way, but it is evident the family has fallen on hard times, and she is quite lovely to look upon. Who knows, perhaps I shall have the opportunity to sample her charms before handing her off to her husband.

I'm going to be visiting the Lady of Derrybrook this evening, as I know for a fact that her husband is not in residence. Although I suspect she will not possess the same sort of gag reflex deficit as your friend from the pleasure house, I can speak from experience that she is commendable in both her grip and enthusiasm.

Please see to it that your reprobate captain is expecting me eventually. I won't demand to have the largest cabin on his ship, only that I have a servant of my own and that I'm free from any seafaring chores he might seek to give me. I do hope those brothel tokens are accepted without expiration.

Yours lovingly,

Silas

By the time he returned to Basingstone from visiting with Lady Derrybrook, dawn was nearly about to break. He felt ready to sleep for a hundred years, trudging up the staircase in the chapel, a twisting spiral of white marble veined in black, the reverse of what he was about to become.

He was eager to return to London, the desire to do so itching at the back of his neck the same way the thought of Miss Eastwick had itched in the back of his mind for half the week. He'd had Lady Derrybrook on her knees, pumping into her from behind, his knot kissing the mouth of her sex insistently when the realization came to him. The lady of the manor was vocalizing her pleasure in a way that brought to mind the ululation of a group of yodelers he'd seen perform at a theater in Paris, the same night he'd taken in a cello concert and performance of a heartrendingly lovely song cycle, sung by a soprano with delicate features and wide brown eyes.

His back arched as the memory coalesced — a vision of Eleanor Eastwick in a long, beaded gown, a spray of feathers in her hair as she sang — and a spray of his seed over the back of Lady Derrybrook, the memory coming to him as he came across her skin, his knot throbbing as his cock jerked, spurting white ropes of his release as he remembered the way Miss Eastwick had kept him and every other attendee of the concert at rapt attention until the last note wavered from her golden throat and applause split the air. Lady Derrybrook wasn't nearly as elegant as she howled at her peak, and Silas slumped, his cock spent and his head heavy.

It was a small miracle he made it back to Basingstone on his feet, and now he wanted to do nothing more than sleep and restore himself, eager to set his affairs in order for the spring season, ensuring Maris had everything she needed as she prepared to deliver her egg.

"Traveling abroad, she said," he mumbled to himself, dropping into his stone throne unceremoniously. The top of the moon chapel was secluded and safe, always a spot of respite, and that night was no exception as the sky lightened. Tomorrow needed to be an extremely productive night, for he had much to do to ensure the manor and his sister were cared for, leaving him free to return to London and the intriguing Eleanor Eastwick.

The High Tea

SOCIETY PAPERS

Dearest readers,

Fresh from the pot, today's brew is a piping hot cup of scandal . . . or is it??

One of London's most libidinous libertine's carriage has been spotted coming and going from an unknown Pimlico address. There appears to be no ball, no dinner, and no celebration afoot . . . so is it a house of ill-repute? Or has one of the ton's sparkling diamonds caught the eye of this stony-hearted rakehell? Only time will tell, my dears, but this reporter will keep an eagle eye on the comings and goings for your benefit!

Until next time —— sip slowly!

Lady Grey

Eleanor

"Is a marquess a higher rank than an earl, Eleanor?"

The twisted edge of her latticed pie was not crimping particularly evenly. Eleanor wasn't entirely sure what she was doing wrong, but after undoing and re-doing the braided dough several times, she still found it to resemble a lumpy sack of boots and gave up. The girls were particular when it came to the parts of a bird they were willing to have on a plate before them, she had learned. If the meat was too dark and oily, Coraline would push it around her plate, building elaborate sculptures in hopes that Eleanor would be satisfied with her architectural ingenuity and not insist she eat. If the shape of the poor fowl was still discernible, Lucy would pretend to swoon, insisting she couldn't possibly bear to eat an innocent little pigeon.

Eleanor wasn't willing to let a single scrap of good meat go to waste, and she had discovered that with the addition of peas and pearl onions and a gravy made from the pan drippings and handful of flour, the girls were far less picky with their pigeon pie the following night. Her pies might not be pretty, but they were obviously palatable, and Lucy and Coraline would both clean their plates without complaint.

Sighing, her eyes rolled up to the ceiling at the question. Lucy had been thoroughly consumed with thoughts of the nobility and their obnoxious visitor since the night he had come for tea. She asked questions about the different titles and stations the nobles held, how lands and titles were passed from son to son, occasionally breaking her educational learnings to sigh over how handsome the Marquis of Basingstone had been. Eleanor had not heard from Silas Stride since that evening he'd come to call, and with each day that passed, she reminded herself and Lucy alike that he had mentioned returning to Basingstone that same week, and besides, the assistance of noblemen was not assured. He was more likely to forget they even existed during his out-of-town absence as he was to come back prepared to assist.

"There's only one way to find out, dear. There's a book on the peerage on the lower shelf there."

"Do you suppose the marquis is also attending the ball, Eleanor? Although," Lucy sighed dramatically, "he's so handsome, I'm certain he already has a betrothed."

Far more likely that he has a different ladies' bedroom he visits every night, with a few brothels thrown in for good measure. Eleanor had done what she felt was her due diligence in looking into the reputation of one Lord Silas Stride. Hettie took the High Tea from the kitchen of the other family she visited each week, leaving them for her grandmother to read over breakfast the following day, and they had amassed a tidy stack of the scandal sheets, handy to use for kindling.

Adroit spectators may have noticed a certain duchess absent from her own soirée for more than just a few passing dances this past weekend. We have it on good authority that her sheets were thoroughly tumbled by a gentleman of rakish repute whose stony heart is no stranger to avid enthusiasts of our piping pot. One wonders if the duke is aware that his bride is paying more attention to the rooftop statuary than to her marital bed.

She had shaken her head in disgust, recognizing the thinly-veiled reference to Lord Stride. And then, only a few issues into the stack was another:

*Eligible gentlemen hoping to land themselves a lady with hair as brilliant as an autumn sunset will have two fewer prospects to choose from this season. When last seen, this pair of identical copper pennies in silk slippers were in a carriage headed to the coast, disgraced after being found in flagrante delicto with a gentleman who was certainly **not** their escort. We have no doubt their devilish partner in this three-backed beast took wing before the early birds, leaving these sulking sisters to face the sun alone.*

He was a scoundrel, a knave, an utter rapscallion, and she was shocked that uncle Efraim would've sent him to her door. Eleanor spent an entire afternoon seething over the implications of each blind item in the High Tea, once she learned the tells they used to signify it was, in fact, Lord Stride. *As someone whose exploits have been regularly and thoroughly excoriated by the High Tea . . .*

"Ugh! Such an *awful* man!" she complained to her hairbrush that morning, remembering the words he himself had uttered regarding his frequent inclusion in the tattler.

She was furious that she was being forced into dealing with someone of such low moral character . . . until she realized that an utter rapscallion was precisely what she needed. After all, she had already been well-trained in the art of pleasant conversation and needlepoint, knew how to sit daintily, and had been instructed in no less than three different ways to sip her tea without slurping. She already excelled at the fairer art of performing the expected coy femininity displayed by young women seeking marriage, and she'd even received a fair education in protecting herself, certainly in protecting her heart.

Attending the conservatory had been a different sort of education. The world of the stage was a treacherous place, after all, full of rivals and rogues and no end to the ways gentlemen sought to find their way beneath a lady's skirt. She had resisted them all in a vain effort to protect her reputation. Now, though, she needed to *acquiesce*, to give in to the same behaviors she'd trained herself so long to resist, and who better to instruct her than a scoundrel.

"It says here that the title of duke and duchess is often reserved for members of the royal family," Lucy read from the book as Eleanor nodded in agreement.

"That's correct, and ducal lands and extensions are often gifted by the crown."

"A marquess is lesser than a duke but higher a title than an earl, count, or baron." Lucy sighed again dramatically. "I don't understand why you have to attend a silly ball at all, Eleanor. Why can't you simply marry the marquis?!"

She didn't bother offering a reply. The question has been asked and answered a dozen times an hour, or at least, that was how it felt. That she would sooner marry the horse seemed not an appropriate answer to give her impressionable sisters.

"Does the marquis know you lived in Paris, Eleanor? Perhaps you'll be able to have a conversation in French since he uses the French designation of his title?" Lucy sighed again, each time a bit more high-pitched than the last. "How romantic that would be!"

"I'm quite certain his designation is from some ancient land treaty and has nothing to do with his own linguistic talent," Eleanor muttered. "He has the same upper-class accent all of the other lords and ladies have; I'm sorry to disappoint."

The girls returned to their studies, and Eleanor returned to focusing on her meal. Dismissing the long-time cook had been a terrible blow. She'd never needed to prepare her own meals before, and learning to do so now, at this stage in life, produced mixed results several times a week on the nights she was forced to do so.

Hettie had turned out to be goddess-sent. A no-non-sense matron from some tiny village in the South, she had filled in the gaps where the other servants were now missing. She picked up light housekeeping duties in addition to her main charge, Eleanor's aged grandmother, and had tacitly given her the name of a part-time cook in another home she visited, a younger girl who would be willing to work for a few shillings several days a week. Between Hettie herself and keeping their carriage, a few shillings was all Eleanor could bring herself to spend, and so the girls had to suffer her lack of culinary skill the other days of the week.

"I can't even begin to tell you how much I appreciate your assistance and discretion, Hettie," Eleanor admitted to the nurse one morning, near tears at having let the fire go out overnight the same week the governess had departed. The older woman had the kindling box smoking in no time, placing the embers in a protective circle until they caught.

"The way I sees it, I'm protecting my interests, miss. It's only a matter of time before you're married off to some rich lordling. Then we'll all be living in a grand house with beautiful scenery and an excellent cook, and I know your character, miss. You won't forget the ones who helped you along the way. So as far as I'm concerned, I'm only ensuring my own retirement plan. If it eases your burden a bit at the same time, maybe it scrubs a bit of soot off my soul."

It was Hettie who came bustling in then, practically dancing across the room to Eleanor, holding out a letter. "Just arrived, miss."

The sight of the wax seal made her stomach flip. The seal bore a snarling gargoyle and was an unusual shade of blue, instantly reminding her of the flashing sapphire of his eyes. Her neck heated as she sliced open the missive. *The Marquis of Basingstone requests the company of Miss Eleanor Eastwick for dinner at his home.* Her eyes scanned the details of when and where, realizing he meant the following night. *A carriage shall arrive to collect you with an appropriate chaperone for the evening.*

Eleanor sagged, feeling dizzy with the emotions crowding her. She was elated that he was helping her and terrified at the prospect of having to endure his company for him to be able to do so. She was shocked that he was at all concerned about preserving her reputation and modesty and blessedly relieved that he was taking the precaution in the first place.

That was, until the following evening.

The chaperone in question was an exhausted-looking mothwoman. Fluffy antennae framed her face, and Eleanor wasn't certain where the fur collar on her pelisse ended, and the thick mantle of fluff around her neck began. A great show was made of the woman coming to the Eastwick's door with the assistance of a footman, her wings a tawny shade of brown, with eyes like an owl's. A bevy of servants descended once they arrived at the marquis's London address, a butler opening the door with a bow, another servant appearing at her elbow to take her coat. She was offered a seat, offered refreshment, and had her every care accounted for before she had even taken five steps beyond the threshold, but there was no sign of Lord Stride in sight.

"His lordship is waiting for you in the conservatory, miss." The mothwoman gestured to another servant, a young woman with huge dark eyes and wings like a dragonfly, leading Eleanor down a long corridor and away from the alleged *chaperone* who was meant to be protecting her virtue. A glance over her shoulder showed Eleanor the sight of the mothwoman dropping into a chair exhaustedly in the room they had just left, her chaperoning duties evidently fulfilled.

He was standing before the glass conservatory walls, overlooking a lovely stone garden. It had begun to drizzle shortly after the carriage had dropped away from the curb in front of her own home, and now the rain came down in a steady patter. The room was lit with candlelight, and between the wavering glow and the syncopation of the rain upon the glass, it lent the conservatory an almost cozy air. Or at least it would have with any other partner.

"Miss Eastwick, you're looking lovely this evening. Truly ravishing."

Her breath caught as he turned to address her, just as striking as he'd been the first time he greeted her. She wasn't sure if he was actually more handsome or if she was being unduly influenced by the fancies of a pre-teen girl, but Eleanor couldn't deny that the Marquis of Basingstone was very easy to look upon. He was tall and slender, despite the breadth of his shoulders and well-formed chest, his form better appreciated in a room of great size like the one they were in. His trousers were just as tightly tailored as they'd been the first night he'd visited, she couldn't help but notice, even though she did try. Once again tucked into high, polished Hessians, the tight fit emphasised the strength in his legs. She had a brief vision of another outline the snug fabric might show her, and her fingers tightened over the top of her beaded reticule in response. *Just remember what a charlatan he is.* Easier said than done as he took her hand to his lips, gazing up from beneath his arched brows in a way that caused a most unladylike swoop in her belly.

"Thank you, my lord. It was most generous of you to send your own carriage to fetch me this evening."

She had fretted endlessly over what to wear, choosing a beaded gown of dusty rose, her hair curled and pinned, uncertain if she was overdressed or underdressed or if it even mattered. Still, the complement *was* mollifying. "I will confess myself a bit confused as to how my chaperone can chaperone from a different room, but I am under your tutelage now, my lord.

The sound of his laughter made her spine shiver, icy white satin against her skin.

"Well, I suppose shedding the inhibitions held by the human gentry is the first step in finding yourself a monstrous mate, my dear. It's very rare that you will find young ladies under such similar constraints amongst the nonhuman population."

"Is it very rare, my lord? Or simply amongst the company you keep?"

Another laugh, the slippery slide of it accompanied by the brush of his fingertips against her back, as he pulled out her chair, and she shivered again.

"Maybe so, Miss Eastwick. You may be right, at that. But I suppose that brings us to our first lesson, one at which I have no doubt you shall excel."

Eleanor glanced around the room pointedly as he seated himself. The conservatory was at once cavernous and intimate. The glassed-in walls gave the space an expansive feel, but the elaborately set table was small, and the candelabras close. The servants beyond the cozy ring of candlelight around them were invisible, as if they dined in some hidden nook, alone together. The very thought brought a blush to her cheeks. "Dinner, my lord?"

Across the table, Silas Stride grinned, his white fangs gleaming in the wavering light. She had a feeling he would be striking no matter what he wore, but based on the two times she had been in his presence, his sartorial choices seemed to favor cool jewel tones, moody blues, and rich violet. That evening was no exception. His waistcoat was a deep aubergine, accented in cranberry, topped off with a blue cutaway coat the color of the night sky. His cravat was as silvery-white as his hair, pinned once more with that plump cherry of a sapphire.

"Witty repartee. Innuendo is an art form, Miss Eastwick. I should remind you that you only have several days to capture and keep the attention of one of the gentlemen at the ball. I understand that humans are quite content to play at being coy indefinitely, but when your time is limited, and a mate is your aim, I assure you, exciting his blood is just as important as your manners. More important, to be quite frank."

Eleanor shifted, discomfited by his words and annoyed that he was right. She did not have the luxury of a full season before her. There would be no endless succession of garden parties and dances, matches of croquet, and afternoons riding. She would have a single weekend to meet, match, and make certain. She needed to exit that weekend with a promise of marriage, and there was no time to fiddle-faddle about pretending she was disinterested.

"Does that mean normal conversation is forsaken in place of suggestion, my lord?"

A graceful lift of a broad shoulder, all the answer required, Eleanor thought.

"Not entirely, no. But I wouldn't get too comfortable ruminating on the restorative properties of the northern cliffs, my dear. Not unless you're doing so with your own natural topography prominently displayed for admiration."

Her cheeks heated, but she held his eye, giving him a tight-lipped smile of her own. "I shall remember to wear my very map, in that case."

"The trick, Miss Eastwick," he continued with a dagger-like grin, "is to make your flirtation as natural as breathing. You don't need to forsake common courtesies, nor does your congeniality need to be derailed completely by double entendres. Let it flow through the course of the conversation."

They were served tableside, her stomach braiding itself in guilt over the fine food and rich wine she was about to enjoy. *And that's why you need to do everything he says. The sooner you can find a husband, the sooner the girls can enjoy fine meals such as this.*

"Are you a fan of the theater, Miss Eastwick?"

His tone was light enough, but she did not fool herself into dropping her defenses. Silas Stride struck her as someone who was always playing a game, and until she knew his rules, she would keep her guard up. "On the rare occasion I have the opportunity to attend, my Lord. My dear father was a great patron of the arts, so our house was always full of music and dancing, and he collected artwork the way some of the gentlemen regularly and thoroughly excoriated in the High Tea seem to collect paramours."

A twitch of his lips, just before they closed over his soup spoon. "And are you well acquainted with such men, Miss Eastwick?"

The first test. She smiled beatifically, carefully lifting her own spoon. "Well, I did accept *your* invitation, did I not, my Lord?"

A toss of his head as he chuckled, low and curling, white hair falling over his forehead in a studied, casual way that was in no way casual at all. She had no doubt he had practiced the move before a mirror several dozen times until he knew exactly how much force the gesture required to make his hair fall as foppishly as it did just then. "I daresay you might be correct in that as well, my dear." A glimmer of fang, the wine steward pulling from the shadows, presenting a bottle for the marquis's approval. "I first had this vintage in Paris, maybe a year or so ago. I bought up several casks soon as I returned home. Have you ever been?"

The hairs at the back of her neck stood up, certain she was being baited. *First, the theater, now Paris. What does he know?* His claws were neatly filed, but she still felt their graze, toying with her as if she were a mouse, trapped before him. Eleanor weighed her options quickly, deciding to come as close to the truth as possible was the best course of action. *The fewer lies you need to keep track of, the less easily he can tangle you in his trap.*

"Yes, my Lord. I received my education in Paris, actually."

"Ah yes, you did mention living abroad. I do hope you had a chance to finish your studies before tragedy brought you home?"

A slow breath, and a fortifying sip of the wine. He was right. It was a very fine vintage. "Yes, I did. By several years. I greatly loved my time in that city, but there are moments now when I wish I could trade back just a few of those years to be closer to my family."

"Sisters, you mentioned?"

The soup bowls were whisked away, and the meat course set before them. Eleanor realized that the intimacy of their table was not imagined, nor was it a trick of the candlelight — there was scarcely room to be had for more than a single course at a time. *You're practically in his lap.*

"Just the two. Lucy is twelve, and Coraline will be nine this summer."

"And will they, too, enjoy the benefit of an education abroad?"

She had just taken a mouthful of pheasant, roasted whole, and then simmered in a decadent cream sauce with buttered neeps, the richest thing she'd tasted in nearly two years. *Richer than anything the girls would ever remember eating, probably.*

Her father had been generous to a fault. His arms and pockets had always been open to friends and loved ones, leading to poor investments and several outright betrayals of his generous heart. If he had still been alive, she had no doubt he would have shoveled them out of the hole the abuses of his finances and good nature cost the family, but left with the girls and no income of her own, nearly empty coffers, and moneylenders sniffing around her door, her sisters would never learn the richness of a meal such as this. *Which is why you will play his silly game.*

"Not at present, my lord," she answered at last, daintily dabbing her embroidered napkin to her mouth. "I have begun hunting for a new governess for them, to be educated at home." She chose not to add that the previous governess had left for lack of payment. "What of your family, Lord Stride?" Eleanor attempted to keep her voice as artificially light as his own. *Turn it back on him, as natural as breathing.* "I confess myself surprised that a lord as handsome and eligible as yourself is not yet married. I regretfully know little of gargoyle culture, but is it not a priority for you or your family? Are you unconcerned with being without an heir?"

His smile hardened out, a tiny flinch she might have missed had she not been staring him down, a thrill of victory rippling beneath her skin. *Have a dose of your own medicine, you smug bastard.*

"I'm certain I have plenty of time to secure my own line of succession, but thank you for your concern, Miss Eastwick. In any case, my sister is carrying her first child, and I've no doubt they will be more than capable of carrying on the family title in the event I prove un-worthy."

She was not expecting him to allude to any sort of un-worthiness, for she never expected any man anywhere to admit that he was ever wrong about anything. She tried to imagine what his sister was like, and wondered if she was just as smirking and haughty.

"Of course," he went on, immediately dispelling any assumption that he wasn't an absolute blackguard of the first order, "I do find the act of marriage a bit daunting. Courtship may seem like a lark, but after the consummation, which is about the only part that interests me, what exactly is left?"

She didn't give him the benefit of her shock at his brazenness, knowing it was what he was after. "If half of what the High Tea writes about you is to be believed, my lord, it seems after consummation, your bride would next be likely to meet . . . well, another man of your own character, I suppose."

Icy white laughter, like a breath of frost, making her wish she'd brought a shawl.

"I suppose that would serve me right, would it not?"

Ignoring his glibness, the unexpected familial disclosure piqued her interest. "How many siblings do you have, my lord?"

"Two. My younger sister Maris, and an elder brother."

It was her turn to raise an eyebrow. *An elder brother? Yet he's the one with the title?* "Forgive me, my lord. Perhaps I'm a bit confused as to how lines of succession work. Your elder brother . . ."

"Is base-born," he finished succinctly. "My father's first wife died shortly after they were married. Mourning in our culture is a lengthy affair, but that did not prevent him from taking a mistress, one who bore him a son. After the appropriate time had been observed, my father remarried, which is how you have the pleasure of dining with me this evening, Miss Eastwick."

"Oh," she whispered. She felt that curious flip-flop in her stomach once more, like a fish on the riverbank, desperate to get back beneath the surface of the water and hide from its lack of courtesy, but before she could apologize, the Marquis continued.

"I do suppose it is a bit uncommon that my brother was raised in the household alongside us," he went on, a half smile curving his lips. "At least until he came of age. My father bought him a commission in the Navy, and that was that. We correspond through letters, but I haven't seen him in several years."

"That's so sad," Eleanor murmured. "I confess, when I lived abroad, it was many months in between seeing my sisters, but my heart ached for them the entire time we were parted."

"Ah yes, that unusual bit of time you spent away from home. I do assume the education you acquired while living abroad to be of a scholarship you were unable to acquire on our own fair shores?"

Eleanor did not like the look he was giving her then, a knowing smirk spreading on his face, recaptured in his claws. *As much truth as you can give.* "I attended the conservatory of music, my lord, and also Sister Winnifred's finishing school for young ladies. But as I said, 'twas hard to be away from those I love."

"And why is it that you are only now seeking a marriage? Forgive me, but it does seem that your first season ought to have been —"

"Quite a few years ago?" she cut in, interrupting him for a change. *Remember what he said. Let the flirtation flow through the conversation. This is a game, and you want to win.* "You're quite right, my lord. I suppose you could say I am a bit of a late bloomer. Although . . . the flowers that bloom last tend to open most fully. Those fair young buds that bloom in spring are often withered and limp by Midsummer, while the late bloomers are still lush" — she held the final *shhh* as if bestowing him a secret — "and resplendent."

He was grinning, and Eleanor had to fight the preposterous inclination to smile back. His look was still penetrating, the drag of his eyes a nearly tangible thing moving down her, but somehow, she felt less discomfited by it that night. *You've already had an opportunity to acclimate to him, plus it's been ages since you've had wine.*

"Still," he persisted, "I do wonder why you waited so long. Unless, of course, you have several seasons already behind you?"

The smile that had been hovering at the corner of her lips hardened as the wine glasses were topped off by the servant who appeared at her elbow. *Don't forget yourself. He's a rude prick.* "This is my very first, my lord. Shocking, I know. My dear father was always incredibly indulgent. I suppose he ought to have listened to my mother and ended my education prematurely to present me to the town sooner." *It's up to you to turn the topic, or else he'll bleat on about your age all night.* "But I suppose it's no more unusual than yourself, Lord Stride, and your lack of a wife."

His eyes glimmered as he raised his wineglass. "I find it thoroughly impossible to choose when there is such a bevy of beautiful and charming young ladies every season. Much as you resemble one of those luscious late-blooming flowers, Miss Eastwick," he purred, his voice clinging to each voluptuous *L*, "I prefer to think of myself as a flitting butterfly, visiting the petals of each beauty in the field."

"Moving from bloom to bloom, my lord?"

"Visiting each to pay homage to their beauty," he agreed, lifting his wineglass to his lips, hesitating with a devilish smirk. "One can hardly hold it against a butterfly for dipping his tongue in for a taste of that sweet nectar."

Heat moved up her neck, capturing her ears and cheeks. *He's testing you. He is a wicked profligate, but you can play this game.* She laughed, a coy trill, watching closely as his fingers moved slowly against the stem of the crystal glass. "What else would the flowers have to discuss, if not the crude attentions of butterflies?" She picked up her own glass, swirling it, watching the garnet liquid circle before continuing. "One does wonder, though, if the purity of butterflies is questioned in the same manner the flowers are judged. After all, a careless butterfly can ruin a delicate bloom as he goes from bud to bud, but who holds him accountable for overused . . . wings?"

His head cocked, the corner of his mouth twitching. He managed to hold his smile in check, but she could see it there in his eyes, and knowledge that *she* had been the one to make those sapphires glimmer was a giddy triumph. She'd never before spoken to a man in such a way, but the theater had been educational in more than just stagecraft.

"On the contrary, my dear, the butterfly merely improves his technique from field to field. All for the betterment of the flower, of course. And those who would judge the flowers so harshly merely want a docile bloom who won't question their lack of mastery over their own" — his hand hung in the air, and she held her breath, wondering if he would be brazen enough to gesture to his lap — "wingmanship."

Do not laugh. Don't give in to his wretched charms. "I hardly see how that is for the betterment of the flowers."

"Oh, but of course it is. A butterfly with skill can land softly upon his chosen flower, giving each luscious petal the attention she deserves." His thumb moved against the crystal stem of his glass, stroking it in a way that made it feel like there were indeed butterflies, all converging in her chest, tickling as his fingers moved up and down. "He will glory in every inch of her, from stem to stamen, with his sweet words," — his thumb stroked down the stem of the crystal, and Eleanor was certain she was able to feel the drag of it down her throat — "his touch," — her nipple tightened as she watched the drag of movement from crystal stem to the curve of the base, the pad of his thumb hugging its voluptuousness. She wondered if he would be pleased with the shape of her breasts or if he would find them too inelegant, a constant fear as she struggled to contain them in dresses she could no longer afford to have cut to her measurements. "And with his tongue," he finished at last, red tongue darting out to touch his lip, as if to prove the point of his mastery. She pressed her thighs together, suddenly feeling flush.

Eleanor thought surely one of the servants must have lit a fire in the grate, for the room seemed uncomfortably hot. The image of Silas Stride's head on the body of a butterfly crossed her mind, a butterfly with miniature dragon wings, like his, flitting from bloom to boom, coming to land on her eventually. Only when he did so, the flower seemed to be growing up from between her spread open-legs, his body covering the blossom of her most intimate place. Fire bloomed in her belly, and she was practically able to feel his clawed hands gripping her legs, the heat of his mouth molten against the petals of her sex.

"When he feeds from her nectar, the dip of his tongue is an ecstasy, Miss Eastwick, not an invasion. She'll open her petals gladly for him and let him have his fill. The finest delicacy a butterfly can enjoy, and with the proper mastery, I assure you, it is extremely pleasurable for the flower."

She could say nothing in response. It was all she could do to remain in her seat and not climb atop the crowded table, pushing pheasant and neeps aside to plate herself before him, raise her skirts and spread her legs wide, and allow Silas Stride to dip his tongue between her thighs. *Why is it so bloody hot in here?!* This was no longer innuendo, Eleanor decided fitfully. He had broken his own rules. As she squirmed in her seat, face flaming, the Marquis of Basingstone raised an eyebrow.

"Surely a lovely flower as yourself has experienced such —"

"I have not, my lord," she answered weakly, wishing it was ladylike to dab at her forehead with her linen napkin. "I'll remind you again, I am but a late bloomer in my first season."

"I do confess myself shocked to hear that, Miss Eastwick. One does hear such tales of far-roaming adventures, after all. I suppose I assumed your time away from home added to your education in this arena."

"Which arena might that be, Lord Stride?" she choked out, the room spinning. "Being a congenial conversation partner? Or tiptoeing around the innuendos of men, holding my tongue one moment and gilding it the next?"

"The arena of actresses, Miss Eastwick."

That careless little shrug again, a thoughtless movement of his broad shoulders, and her heart sank. She was never going to get her family out of this sinking morass in which they'd been left.

"Conventional wisdom says," he went on in that lofty, careless tone, "that a lady of the stage is not much different from a lady of the night, does it not?"

"Conventional wisdom is often wrong, I assure you." She felt overheated and dizzy, her head ached, and her appetite for both the rich food before her and the gargoyle across the table was gone. "Conventional wisdom would have me believe you to be a gentleman, Lord Stride, and not the unrepentant rake that you are." *It was a mistake coming here. It was a mistake trusting him at all.*

"You're blushing so a*dor*ably I'm inclined to believe you," he chuckled, his voice a bit incredulous. "Are you a virgin, Miss Eastwick?"

There was no sense in lying, not anymore. She didn't know how he found her out, but he had, thoroughly, and she wasn't helping herself any further by continuing to obfuscate the truth any more than she was helping herself by listening to him. Eleanor shook her head.

"No, my Lord." Silas Stride said nothing, but he raised an icy eyebrow, giving her space to continue for a change. "I was sixteen, about to leave for the conservatory. I was terrified," she remembered, tears stinging at the corner of her eyes. "Young women are told such *wretched* things about what will happen to us in our marital bed. I was even more afraid to go off on my own, away from the protection of my family. I just wanted to get it over with, so I wouldn't have this horrible thing, this fear, hanging over me."

"And was it an enjoyable experience?"

She choked out a bitter laugh, tears spilling over her lashes. It didn't make a difference. She was already humiliated, she decided. "It was not. He was also sixteen, one of our stable boys. It hurt. The only thing it had to recommend itself was that it was over very quickly."

The Marquis of Basingstone leaned forward on his elbows, that searching look back in his eye. "And you've not had a lover since then?" His brow furrowed when she shook her head again. "One hears such tales of patrons. If you did not take a lover, then who . . ." His head tipped back, smile splitting as he chuckled again. "Lord Ellingboe."

"Yes," she whispered, nodding. "Uncle Efraim gave me patronage for the duration of my study. After I left the conservatory, I performed in some small theaters while I completed finishing school at Sister Winnifred's."

He laughed then, a slip of satin against her back, making her shudder. "I was wracking my brain to think of how I knew you, Miss Eastwick, for several days. And then I remembered. Your voice is exquisite, as lovely as your face." He sat back in his chair, giving her an appraising look. "An actress, nearly as pure as a rose. Who would've believed it? All things considered, my dear, you are quite skilled in verbal seduction. No doubt learned at the stage door, attempting to put off your would-be suitors."

"Quite right," she bit out, deciding she'd had enough. He'd been toying with her from the start and had no idea if his offer of assistance would even still stand now that the truth was out. "You are right that verbal seduction is an art form, but so too, my lord, is flattery. It's not proper to employ in civilized settings, for example, at Lady Farthington's Ball, but well used in a one-on-one situation. Isn't that what all you men want? Butterflies flitting from flower to flower, eager to be told how handsome you are, how witty you are, what a fine hunter and horseman and banker you are? You're

quite right that I became extremely skilled at word-
play and flattery, extricating myself from situations and
conversations with men like you. Lords and dandies
who only want to ruin women, ruin our reputations and
our virtue. Flattery, I discovered, was the best way to
put those men off, and I can't imagine it wouldn't work
on you as well, Lord Stride. You now have the power to
ruin me for London society. Is that enough? How long
am I expected to stroke your ego before I've sufficiently
mollified your colossal vanity, my lord?"

Silas Stride was positively beaming at her across the
small, intimate table, and she realized that, too, had
likely been a design of his making. "And a show of
temper for the finish," he crowed. "Miss Eastwick, you
didn't even allow me to give the instruction for that!
A bit of flirtation, some carefully applied innuendo, a
spat to whet the appetite, and then enjoying each other
for dessert. If you do at the ball exactly as you've done
tonight, my dear, you'll have your pick of suitors. I don't
know about my ego, but it's not the only thing that
could do with a good bit of stroking right about now."

She gasped, nearly choking on her shock, clapping her hand over her mouth, shoulders shaking.

"Does-does this mean you still intend to help me, my Lord?"

His wings rustled behind him, huge leathery things, the same raven black of his skin, shot through with white veining. They were tipped in curved horns, exactly like a dragon, and she thought again of him flitting across the field of flowers, alighting on her, and using his tongue in the most sinful way she could imagine.

"Of course, Miss Eastwick, I gave you my word. And aside from that, the Ellingboes are family friends, and I would not disrespect the earl by turning down his request. This *does* change things, though."

Despite her flush, Eleanor shivered. "Does it?"

"It does," he intoned flatly. "I was operating on the assumption you had some experience in the carnal arts. I myself have no use for virgins, and in practical application, Miss Eastwick, that is essentially what you are." He held up a hand to stave off her sputter of outrage. "Yes, I am well aware that is the expectation of well-bred young ladies. I daresay most of your rivals at the ball will come boasting the same inexperience. That doesn't help *you*, though."

He pursed his lips in consideration, tipping his head back in thought, providing her the perfect vantage to admire his sharp bone structure. His face was a series of extreme angles — high, jutting cheekbones, a sharp jaw, and a straight nose. His eyebrows, too, were acutely arched, and as she ogled him, he tapped a shaped claw to his wide mouth.

"You're certainly beautiful, Miss Eastwick. Despite the fact that you dress like a matron of eighty years, you're quite lovely to behold."

She sputtered again, the unexpected criticism coming wrapped in a compliment, like a refreshing glass of lemonade that squirts unceremoniously in the eye.

"You have impeccable manners," he went on, unconcerned over her offense, "and you're a charming, if not a bit audacious, conversation partner. I've sat witness to your talent, and your determination to make a good eventual match for your sisters speaks to a generous heart and sacrificial nature. But it takes more than pretty songs and words to find a man willing to call himself your husband, Miss Eastwick. And these aren't mere men, after all. Their *appetites* will need satisfying."

She flushed at the implication. *What have you gotten yourself into?*

"One cannot underestimate the necessity of an education in the art of pleasure, particularly when time is of the essence. You've less than a month, my dear. You will need to please whichever lordling sets his sights upon you, and I won't have you besmirch my good name as a lover of repute by being completely ignorant in how to do so." When he turned his gaze back to her at last, his eyes were positively wicked, sinful sapphires glimmering in the candlelight. "Your lessons will be on the art of seduction and lovemaking, Miss Eastwick. You've much to learn, and who better to teach you than an unrepentant rake?"

By the time she was back in her own bed that night, a little felt as if she'd been set up on hot coals, smoking from the inside out. She tossed and turned fitfully, falling her fists at her side in aggravation, uncertain how she was meant to go to sleep with fire bubbling in her veins.

When he'd risen from the table, the shape of his cock stood out in relief within his tight trousers. He was hard, and the realization that *she* had been the one to cause the reaction in him made her heat at the time, press a giddy hand to her mouth on the carriage ride home, and now she writhed beneath her sheets.

Everything he said was true. She was, for all intents and purposes, a virgin in all practical matters of sensuality. She had likely seen more than most, thanks to the theater. Patrons were shameless with their hand-picked favorites, and so too were the couples backstage, ballerinas and musicians and stagehands, all coming together to find a place to come together.

She had watched — from a hidden vantage point in the flies, where she had stopped to eat her lunch – the costume mistress on her knees before the rehearsal conductor, suckling his cock tip as he groaned. She had happened upon chorus girls being rutted from behind by their patrons and stagehands lazily stroking themselves, but she had never been a party to it. She had no idea what to do, what to say, how to go about initiating or receiving . . . But she had made Silas Stride's cock grow stiff, barely even meaning to.

There was going to be no sleeping that night, not unless she extinguished these licking flames that were practically cramping her stomach. Closing her eyes,

Eleanor skated her nails down her body, pulling up her night rail with her lip caught between her teeth.

When he feeds from her nectar, the dip of his tongue is an ecstasy, Miss Eastwick. She tried to imagine what it might feel like, her monstrous husband, if he, too, would have clawed hands, horns, or wings, or if he would have the towering stature of an orc, or the slithering tail of a serpent. She imagined the drag of neatly manicured claws down the front of her thin night rail, cupping her full breasts and catching at her hardened nipples. She wondered if she would feel the drag of his fangs against her stomach, if he would push open her legs slowly. She had seen this act only once, but once had been enough to emblazon it upon her mind, a memory she had revisited over and over again over the years. Lord Stride's vivid butterfly metaphor insinuating the same act had left her aching.

Eleanor tried to imagine his hot breath against her petals, blossoming open with the heat of his mouth and the stroke of his tongue. She slid a finger through her silky slick folds, imagining that it was his tongue doing so instead. *With the proper mastery, I assure you, it is extremely pleasurable for the flower.* She had no doubt that he would be a master at his sinful craft, moving her fingers to stimulate the flutter of a butterfly's wings, the flicking of his tongue against her most sensitive part, that aching little pearl she had discovered quite on accident in the bath and now revisited only beneath the privacy of her bed sheets. He would know just how to move his tongue, she was certain. He would lick her, dipping his tongue in her taste, stroke her with its heat, and suckle it with his lips.

Silas Stride was a rake and a rogue and an unrepentant profligate, and she would be glad to be rid of him once the ball was over. But there was no question that he would be a skilled lover, able to bring her to ecstasy. She had extricated a promise from his lips before she had climbed into the carriage that night — that his instruction would be academic, theory and technique, but not practical application. He had laughed, shrugging again with an expansive gesture.

"Whatever you wish, Miss Eastwick. We shall do our best in any case."

That was the smart thing to do. Let him teach her what she would need to know to please her husband, what she would need to do at the ball to catch his eye, whoever he might be, excite his blood, and stiffen his cock. It would be for him to teach her beyond that, whoever her monstrous mate would be.

But Silas Stride would make her scream. All of those women, those titled women with so much to lose, they wouldn't keep allowing him in their beds if he wasn't a skilled lover. Her hips left the mattress, rising to meet her hand, his tongue, the heat of his mouth. When the tension within her broke, Eleanor pressed her fist against her teeth, swallowing her moan.

She couldn't stand him. He was rude and smug and entirely too pleased with himself, and she would be glad once his instruction was over and she was married, all of her problems laid to rest. Until then, though, allowing the Marquis of Basingstone to give her hands-on lessons in lovemaking might not be the worst idea she had ever allowed herself to be talked into. She sunk into the pillow, pushing away the troubling thought, the sound of his cold laughter, and the mischievous glow of his dark blue eyes. She only had to get through a few more weeks, and then this would all be over.

Silas

Eleanor Eastwick was a vexation; one of whom he'd be glad to be rid of soon enough.

The second time he had visited her in her home, all three of the other ladies of the house were eager to present themselves — the two children, of whose presence he was aware, and an agéd grandmother, who had not been mentioned previously. He might have been a libertine of the highest order, but poorly mannered he was not, and it took little effort on his part to charm the two young ladies as well as the older matron.

His eyes had wandered around the room as the young girls recited a poem for his benefit, picking out a spot on the floor where the wood was darker, denoting a piece of furniture that had long stood there. From its odd shape and his hostess's musical education, he guessed a piano. Silas did not like the twist in his stomach when his gaze moved from the empty spot to Eleanor Eastwick's quickly downcast eyes, as if she were watching him looking and knew exactly what it was he would see. The library, too, seemed somewhat emptier to him than it had been the first night he met her, graciously accepting the glass of port he'd been offered as the younger girls went to bed.

"I hope you don't mind an old lady like me being your chaperone this evening, my lord," the old dowager had chided gaily as Eleanor went to tuck the girls in. He decided not to take it as an affront to his charm that she was already dozing in her chair by the time Miss Eastwick returned, reminding him of what a strain on the family his visits likely were.

"I do apologize, Miss Eastwick. I'm sure it's frightfully inconvenient for you to play hostess at this time of night."

She'd shrugged prettily, topping off his glass and pouring herself two fingers of the rich liquid, grinning at his raised eyebrow. "If I'm to have a cup of ratafia, my lord, you will be having one as well. And as I told you once before, Lord Stride, I'm a bit of a night owl. Always have been. I assure you, these hours are quite normal to me."

Something moved inside him at her admission, a queer shift in his chest that left him feeling slightly out of breath, and he worried he was forming some condition. Of course, she would be used to late hours, he reminded himself. How many times had he left the concert halls and theaters, arriving at some private salon for a post-theater sup at near midnight? The performers at such venues would be doing the same, a celebratory drink and meal with cast and crew mates at taverns or else leaving on the arm of a wealthy patron for a private party. *She's more apt to keep your hours than half your staff.*

"Do you know why I so enjoy the theater, Miss Eastwick?" he asked suddenly, watching her eyebrows raise. "I keep an apartment in Paris for much the same reason as I keep a permanent residence in London, you know. Partially for business but mostly because I do so enjoy patronizing the arts. Symphonies and operas, theaters that produce concerts and plays and exhibitions, like the one where I heard you sing. They all have one thing in common, my dear. They're designed to be enjoyed at night."

Her eyes were bright, her full lower lip trapped between her teeth in a gesture he was beginning to recognize as familiar, something she did unconsciously. *It's a poor way to treat such a lovely little lip.* "There is much in this world I do not experience," he went on, forcibly pulling his eyes from her inviting mouth. "Things of which I only know of through tales and books and illustrations . . . but sitting in a crowded room and hearing an incomparably lovely soprano singing of loss and heartache is not a pleasure to be undertaken in the afternoon. So I suppose the existence of lovely nightingales such as yourself are the trade-off for a lifetime in the dark." Silence stretched between them for several long, yawning moments after his uncharacteristic disclosure, but it was strangely comfortable, and he had no desire to fill the space with chatter.

"You know, now that you mention it," she said after a moment, leaning forward in her seat, "it was a bit odd discussing flowers and butterflies with someone who is stone throughout the day, my lord."

The genuine bark laughter that escaped him at her words was startling. *Definitely coming down with something.* He was so used to the sound of his own icy affectation, and it had been too long since someone made him laugh in a way that caused a stitch in his side, possibly not since Cadmus had last visited. *What was in this port? Are you drunk?!*

The entire situation was such an unusual tableau to find himself within — a silent home at night with sleeping children, all candles and lamps extinguished except the ones surrounding them, their quiet conversation taking place in a room partially devoid of furniture with a septuagenarian snoring lightly in the corner. There were no half-naked duchesses lying about, no countess on her knees before him with cum-smeared lip rouge, and no empty wine bottles to be found. There was only this girl, with her quiet dignity and hideous dress and her singular ability to make him behave completely out of character.

"Do you know, I have no bloody idea what I'm talking about most of the time?" he continued to laugh, attempting to stifle himself and failing miserably. Eleanor was wheezing with an unladylike lack of restraint, pressing her mouth into the crease of her arm. "I don't know that I've ever even seen a butterfly. Pinned, of course, and in pictures, paintings . . . Ah," he harrumphed triumphantly with a start, raising a finger to herald his reversal of fortune in the conversation as she shook with laughter. "If we were to reframe our earlier conversation with the use of moths instead, Miss Eastwick, I should be back on even footing with you."

She had continued to laugh like a crystalline bell, and the words were out of his mouth before he could give it the thought it should've surely required.

"Have you ever been kissed, Miss Eastwick?"

She sputtered in the candlelight as soon as he asked the question, cheeks heating, giving her peaches-and-cream skin a berry flush. He wasn't sure why he had initially thought the girl capable of the sort of tempestuous behavior expected of ladies of the stage. He could bring a blush to her cheeks with hardly any effort, so adorably naïve she was the actual act of lovemaking. The act itself, he corrected, for she was certainly no stranger to the mechanics of it, ruefully admitting that she had seen her fair share of scandalous sights in her theater days.

"Not in the way I'm certain you're thinking of, my lord," she sniffed at last, tilting her nose in the air, attempting to reclaim the dignity his question had momentarily robbed.

This would be her first lesson, he decided, pushing to his feet. "There's nothing complicated to it, my dear. You merely press your lips to the lips of another." His eyes followed her lip, sucked between her teeth once more. He was going to give the plump little cushion the care it deserved after such shoddy treatment by its owner.

Eleanor laughed uneasily, hands fisting in her dress as she rose nervously. "I suspect it's a bit more than that." Her lip caught between her teeth again as he shrugged, taking a step closer.

"I suppose it is. But we all must start somewhere, and you can't progress without mastering the basics."

He was able to feel her soft intake of breath, a quick suck inward as he bent, just before his lips pressed to hers, learning their warmth and softness. He did nothing more than press his mouth to hers, as promised. *At least for now.* She was gasping when they parted, the consequence of not breathing for the duration.

"Am I correct in assuming that humans have functioning airways, Miss Eastwick?" he asked dryly with a roll of his eyes. "Breathing, I don't feel like I should have to say, is essential. If you asphyxiate on your prospective mate before he has a chance to offer a proposal of marriage, what is even the point of all this?"

Her eyes had narrowed, shoulders straightening, and he had been forced to duck his head to hide his smile. She was a proud little thing, determined to do everything on her own, and he knew the family must be in dire straits if she had deigned to seek his help in the first place.

"Alright, let's. . ." Glancing around the room, he snuffed several tallow candles, frowning at the two rushlights he'd not previously noticed. Eleanor's grandmother was cast into deeper shadows, more comfortable for the older woman to sleep by, he told himself. When he turned, the sight of Miss Eastwick standing there, the decreased illumination making her eyes seem even more luminous, made his cock jump against his thigh and a repeat of that strange tightening in his chest. "Let's sit," he murmured, angling the chairs to sit at far-closer-than-proper proximity.

"My heart is racing," she admitted with a small laugh in a strained voice, allowing him to pull her to a chair before seating himself beside her.

"There's no cause to be nervous, Miss Eastwick. Far better to get over your trepidation now when you're not vying for the attention of a suitor you've only just met. And look — technically, you're not without a chaperone."

He took advantage of her small laugh to lean in, pressing his lips gently to hers once more. For several long heartbeats, that's all he did. A gentle press, pull back, another gentle press until he was confident she was breathing. "Not so challenging, is it?"

Her eyes were closed, but she shook her head, already leaning in, and the next press of his mouth to hers. He wanted to suck that plump little lip in between his own and lave it with his tongue, an apology for how often she gripped it between her teeth. He felt her gasp of surprise against his own breath when he did so, her fists gripping great handfuls of her skirt. Silas lost track of how long he spent softly kissing her in the near dark. All he knew was that every time he parted his lips ever so slightly, she would gasp, and his cock would jump. Finally, he decided they needed to progress.

"And now we deepen it a bit, Miss Eastwick."

Her eyes were still tightly closed when he let his tongue move over that abused little lip. Stroking at the seam of her mouth until her lips parted in shock, inadvertently granting him entrance.

"Am I to be using my tongue in such a way as well, my lord?" she gasped, lifting her head to take a deep shuddering breath.

"Eventually. Eventually, you'll want to. But it's alright if you let me do the work for now, my dear." At the first stroke of his tongue against hers, Silas was positive his cock had begun to vibrate. When he had his fill of her mouth and trailed down to nibble at her neck, her head dropped back with her mouth open in shock, and his cock began to throb. He wanted to lift her hand and place it on the solid bulge at the front of his breeches; wanted to let her feel how she inflamed him. Instead, he led her hand to his jaw, shivering against her when her nails scraped at the skin behind his long ear, her fingers pushing into his hair without needing to be led.

When at last they parted, Eleanor was gasping, laughing as she held her head. "Is it supposed to make you this dizzy?"

"What did I tell you, Miss Eastwick? Nothing to worry about. You're a fine pupil."

The change in her was instantaneous. She sobered, straightening in her chair, blinking up at him for several moments before she nodded. "That was quite the informative lesson, my lord."

When their mouths came back together, everything was different. She was more active in participating — following his cues, moving her tongue against his and catching his lips with her teeth, playing the part of the perfect seductress. He hated it.

He was agitated once he left the Eastwick residence a short while later. Stretching his wings, he climbed to the roof far earlier than needed, deciding to jump from the parapet and hope the wind would catch him. *And if not, you'll fall and break your neck, and that might be for the best.* The wind had caught, though, giving him an opportunity to use his wings in a way he hadn't in weeks, working out some of the frustration and pent-up energy her kiss had ignited within. By the time he took his place on the roof before sunset, his head ached and his cock was still hard, jutting out like a handle as he dropped his banyan aside.

Eleanor Eastwick vexed him, and the Monster's Ball couldn't come soon enough, Silas decided that morning, staring into the horizon, waiting for the moment when he stiffened, skin hardening to smooth marble.

Perhaps he was merely coming down with something, he told himself. That would explain his mood and the odd shift in his chest, and the unsettled way he was feeling. He would need to ensure he took an especially sunny spot for the next few days, soaking up the restorative powers of the sun as best he could, the better to clear his mind. Clear his mind, and shake away the cobwebs she cast there, lest he tangled himself in her web.

"Remember, Miss Eastwick, the steps are secondary."

The musicians hired to play for them that evening consisted of two goblins and a disgruntled-looking troll, but their fiddles were merry, which was all that mattered. The end of the ballroom where they danced was lit with more than a dozen candelabras, the most obvious display of their different circumstances that could possibly be.

It was her third visit to his home, and Kestin's sister Cressida was once again serving as the most permissive chaperone in England. She'd easily been persuaded to take on the job, knowing fully well that it meant she could enjoy a night off with her feet up, all of the house-keeping duties foisted onto other hands for the evening. The mothwoman had likely gone to take a nap the instant Eleanor was safely delivered over the threshold.

"Secondary? What are you talking about?! The steps are incredibly important!" she laughed in outrage, stamping a slippered foot. "You're going to have me fall on my face and look a fool!"

"You are not dancing to show off your dancing skill," Silas went on severely, ignoring her adorable outburst. "This is, first and foremost, an opportunity for you to be physical with your potential suitor in a socially acceptable way. Don't undervalue the positioning of your body, and don't allow your focus on *choreography*," the last said with a sneer, "to impact your allure."

They began a moment later, a bow and a curtsey, and then they were off, lightly hopping steps, coming together as they crossed through the center of the marked-off dancing square. Despite their height difference, his hands landed on her hips easily. They moved through all positions of the quadrille, assuming the role of all four couples, and she was laughing by the end, clapping for the musicians and attempting to catch her breath.

"I did not expect you to be so light on your feet, my lord. You're a very fine dancer."

"Yes, Miss Eastwick, this is not my first ball; I'll have you know. You are a most graceful dancer yourself, but I'll confess I would have preferred you to have all the terpsichorean skill of a calf in a field if it meant you wouldn't be focusing solely on your feet."

"I am sorry that you find my sole focus on my soles so distressing, my lord," she tittered as he took her by the waist, leading her back into position. "I shall try to do better this time."

By the third circuit they danced together, she was a preening vixen. Stretching her arms out as if she had wings of her own, she glanced up over her shoulder at him coyly, eyes sparkling as he took her gloved hands. She arched her back against him like a cat when they came together briefly, his hands at her hip as he turned them into the next movement, and her own hands stroked his arms as he held her through the steps.

By the time the music changed, the opening strains of a waltz replacing the bouncy quadrille, she was giggling and he was stiff, his trousers fitting more snugly than they had only just at the start of the dance.

"Do you know how to waltz, Miss Eastwick?"

"In theory, my lord. It's quite scandalous, is it not? To dance so close?"

Silas pulled her against him, hand dropping to her lower back, pressing her to his front, his eyes fluttering at the pressure against his erection. Opening his wings fully, he beat the air once, twice, satisfied with the number of candles that snuffed, shielding them from any keen eyes the musicians may have possessed.

"My dear Miss Eastwick," he purred in her ear, "the scandal is the point."

Unlike the quadrille, there was no hopping and shifting in the waltz. She was a graceful enough dancer that she fell into the step easily, following his lead, and he led her in such a way that kept her anchored against him, bodies flush. It was indeed a scandal — a scandal that he could not ravish her right there in the middle of the empty ballroom, no one to hear her moans but the well-paid musicians who could be kept discreet for enough coin. By the time the music came to a close, he ached with longing, and she clung to his jacket as if she might fall without his support.

He wanted her. There was little sense in denying it. He wanted to have her beneath him, legs around him, fingernails scoring his chest and her teeth at his neck; wanted her on her knees, helpless and keening as he rutted into her from behind, his knot swollen and kissing the lips of her cunt. He wanted to dip his tongue into the sweet nectar between her thighs and wanted to see her heavy-lidded gaze as she looked up at him, his cock in her mouth. He wanted to claim every part of her before she left for her ball, before another beast would have her. He wanted her before she became lady so-and-so to, forever tethered to another noble. He was desperate to have her, and in doing so, wasn't he actually helping the girl? Wasn't this part of the education he had promised her? The art of seduction? The ability to turn any of the monstrous noblemen at the ball into putty in the palm of her hand?

In any case, she did not put up any resistance as he turned her out of the ballroom into a smaller salon at the back of the house, empty and dark, save for the moonlight that spilled in from the glass doors, overlooking a small balcony — perfect for an illicit tryst.

"Are you feeling better prepared, Miss Eastwick?" he asked, lifting her as if she were a doll, landing on a backless chaise lounge with her half in his lap. "We're only a little more than two weeks away now." The only answer he received was her gasp, just before his lips met hers savagely. Her fingers raked through his hair as he kissed down her jaw, gasping what his fangs caught at her sensitive earlobe. Silas felt a ripple down his back as she stroked the base of one of his horns with her nails, and the cry that broke from her throat as he pressed his mouth to the top of her breasts was like a lightning bolt to his cock.

She had dressed for dancing — a scoop-necked gown with short, puffed sleeves, and the temptation to free her breasts was too great for him to ignore. She was fuller-busted than was fashionable, and he could tell by the small, unconscious adjustments she made to her clothing — constant little tugs, pulling at her neckline, straightening her waistline — that she was self-conscious over her ample assets. She needn't have worried, for she was always adequately covered in her oddly unfashionable wardrobe. They may have been a source of self-consciousness for her, but they had been an object of lust for him since the moment he bent to kiss her hand that very first night, imagining their softness. He wanted to bury his face into the pillowy mounds of flesh, wanted to kiss and suck and tease her nipples with his tongue, and there was no time at all, he decided, like the present.

"I have wanted to kiss these luscious breasts since the very first night you had me to tea, Miss Eastwick," he growled against her. "I do hope that whatever wardrobe you have planned for the ball, it shows them off as the glories they are."

She squealed when he pulled at the neckline of her dress, her body arching against him, freezing when he pulled a creamy globe free. "My lord," she gasped, her nails scrabbling his shoulders. Silas hesitated, wanting to ascertain that he had her permission to continue before going any further.

"Do you want to further your education this evening, my dear, or would you prefer to call it a good night?" He punctuated his words with a tongue against the peaked nipple before his mouth, a long, hot lick, followed by the cool air of him blowing gently, his balls throbbing as she moaned at the sensation. "The choice is yours, Miss Eastwick. I don't wish to pressure you into something you'll regret. This is an education in pleasure, not a lecture on force."

"Just—just a few minutes longer, my lord," she panted. "But please, no further than this. At least . . . not just yet."

"As you wish, my dear. And if you want to stop, we stop."

Her nails traveled down the back of his head as he spoke, scraping through his hair and down his neck until they reached the collar of his coat, an insufferable impediment that he wanted to cast off along with his waistcoat and shirt, kicking his fine leather boots out the window, and setting fire to the tourniquet of his trousers. He wanted to shred her dress with his claws, free her of her stays and shift; wanted to leave her in nothing but her long gloves and pendant necklace, naked beneath him.

"Absolutely stunning," he murmured against her breast, sucking her nipple into the hot cavern of his mouth and suckling like a babe as she mewled against him. She smelled like lilac water and fresh cream, soft and sweet, and very much wanted to spend the duration of the evening exactly where he was. "You're going to be leaving me in quite a state, Miss Eastwick," he rumbled once he released the swollen bud with a *pop*.

"W-what do you mean?" she gasped out, keening as his fangs dragged against her skin.

Silas took her hand, stroking her small fingers, kissing her knuckles reverently, and nuzzling his nose to her wrist . . . before placing her open palm against the straining shape of his rock-hard cock at the front of his trousers. "See what you've done to me, little moth?"

Eleanor struggled to sit up, as if she wanted to *see* what she'd just felt, her cheeks reddening when she did so. She allowed him to place her hand on his bulge once more, slowly dragging her nails over the shape of his tumescence, squeezing until he grunted against her. So snug were his trousers and so swollen was his cock, that she was able to press the tip of her nail to the thick root that ran up the underside of his shaft with ease, finding and tracing a snaking vein with a feather-light pressure that left him panting. Her gaze flickered from the shape of his erection to his heavy-lidded eyes, lip sucked between her teeth as she gave him another tentative squeeze.

"That's it, darling. Just like that. If you tease your suitor half so well, you'll be likely to have a proposal before dinner on the second night."

When she reached the ribbed ridges at the base of his head, she hesitated, sucking in a shuddering breath before letting her nails continue to trace and scrape. His cock was throbbing, his knot fully inflated, and he was overcome with the desire to flip their positions, push it into her, and spend himself, stoppering her cunt like a cork as he pumped her full of his hot seed. He had never knotted a woman before, refusing to be saddled with the responsibility of children who could not even inherit his title, the ill-thought consequences of unguarded lust — but he was desperate to knot Eleanor Eastwick, the desire to do so making him dizzy. When her fingers ran over the apple-sized knot at the base of his shaft, it was his turn to groan, the sound swallowed by the soft pillow of her naked breast.

"Is-is this a-a —"

"A slight difference in our anatomy," he gritted out, wheezing as she explored the swollen protuberance. "One that's" — she squeezed, and Silas felt his eyes roll back with a force that nearly blinded him —"extremely sensitive to pressure, as you just applied. It's to aid in breeding, although I've only ever found use for its more pleasurable applications."

Her hand slowed, nails scraping in a way that made his back arch. "Do you go into a-a *breeding* heat, my lord?"

Her voice was hushed, and Silas could not immediately tell whether or not she sounded horrified or intrigued at the notion. He was almost disappointed to have to answer in the negative. Eleanor Eastwick's hand dragged up the length of him, her eyes intent, student outrunning the teacher, and he nearly choked on his grunt of pleasure.

"I do not, but the females of my species do. Fortunately, I'm not terribly interested in placing myself in a position where that would make a difference."

"And is this such a place, my lord?" Another squeeze to his knot, slow and deliberate. Her finger began to pulse, palpating him until his heartbeat matched the cadence, thudding at the back of his tongue and behind his eyes. The desire to cover her body with his and claim her as his own was making him dizzy. "That is, one of the scenarios you *do* place yourself within?"

Silas struggled to meet her lips, crashing his mouth to hers, claiming her with lips and teeth and tongue, the same way he wanted to claim her body. He felt her quick intake of breath, her hand squeezing the shape of him as he stroked his tongue against her own, and finally, her soft sigh of acquiescence as she melted into the kiss, surrendering. She was hardly the first woman he'd had in such a position, but Silas couldn't deny that the weight of her in his arms and the long press of her body to his was singularly delicious.

"This is a far more desirable position than I normally find myself in, my dear. Perhaps you would care for us to adjourn upstairs and continue your lesson in more comfortable surroundings?"

Her hands faltered at his words, releasing him entirely before pulling away slowly. She blinked down at him as she sat up, her chest heaving. "Yes, of course," she gasped out. "My lesson. It's good of you to keep reminding me, Lord Stride."

The sound that came then from the hallway was so calamitous and unexpected that they both jumped, Eleanor crying out in surprise. In the blink of an eye, her dress was righted and smoothed, beautiful creamy breasts tucked away where they belonged, her hair patted back into place, and the look on her face only a tiny bit guilty.

"I-I should go, my lord. It's getting quite late. Thank you for the valuable instruction."

Silas wanted to argue, wanted to remind her that these late hours were normal for her, she'd said. That she was nearly like him — a creature of the twilight. She should stay, spend the rest of the night with him, stay with him until dawn and let him pleasure her until his skin was stiff and unyielding . . . It made no difference. She left quickly after the unceremonious interruption — which had been one of the musicians dropping their case — looking away as he kissed her hand, her eyes downcast and her cheeks flushed. *And here you are, old boy — cock throbbing and not a soul to care.*

"Will you sing for me?"

He was smiling as she turned. They had just finished taking tea in the conservatory again. It was his favorite room in the London house. The closest he could get to being out-of-doors while still safely ensconced, the moonlight shining down upon them.

There was much debate amongst his kind, whether they were creatures of the sun, creatures of the moon. They took their energy from the sun, absorbed heat and life, soaking it in from sunrise to sunset, but beneath the moon's icy gaze, they came alive. Silas didn't feel any particular affinity for the sun. He had never seen it, so he didn't miss it. The moon, though, the moon he loved and could never get enough. Sitting beneath the glass ceiling of the conservatory across from Eleanor Eastwick in the middle of the night, the moon shining down on them, felt unbearably comfortable. *Too* comfortable.

It was a heavy pressure that clawed at his insides, pulling him down until he didn't know whether or not he wanted to surrender beneath it or struggle against it. There was that strange shift again in his chest as he watched her daintily sip from her cup – so lovely to behold, well mannered, well bred, pauperized by life's cruelties, beyond her control, and his arms twitched, aching to take her. If he learned that Eleanor Eastwick was a witch, Silas would not be at all surprised. His arms, his chest, his grasping hands — they all longed to pull her under the sensation with him, and it was only his good sense that kept him upright.

Now she stood across the room, looking out the glass wall to the garden courtyard beyond, but her expression as she turned made his own smile falter. She looked stricken. Some nameless emotion crossed over her face, darkening her eyes and making her smile resemble a grimace. Silas had no idea what it was or what caused it, only that he had the peculiar impulse to kiss it away and banish it forever.

"I'm likely to be a tad too rusty for that, my lord." She'd recovered well enough, but her smile was strained, and her eyes downcast.

"I highly doubt that. I remember your performance that night in Paris. You are magnificent. There was a table of ladies next to me, and all three of them were sniffling. I won't require an elaborate opera scene, merely a —"

"Please don't ask it of me."

The misery in her voice, cutting him off, made the words die in his mouth. Her eyes were bright with tears, and he nearly swallowed his clumsy tongue. His feet moved without his permission, crossing the room to her in two long strides, pulling her into his arms.

"Don't sully these lovely cheeks with tears, my dear. I can't bear to see you look so melancholy."

She turned against him, pressing her face to the place where his heart was tripping in his chest, and he wondered if she could feel its uneven syncopation. It was an inappropriate position, too familiar, too close, and not nearly close enough. Silas took the opportunity to lower his face to her hair. Lilac water, soft and lovely, the singular smell of her skin beneath, the sweetest thing he'd ever smelled in his life.

"Why does something that brought you so much joy now bring only sorrow, my lovely Miss Eastwick?"

For a long moment, she said nothing. Shaking her head slowly, her eyes pressed closed, tears trapped between the fringe of her dark lashes. "That's not my life anymore. It won't ever be again. I won't ever sing like that again. I won't ever perform again. I'll probably never see Paris again. My parents will never be alive again. There's no sense in living in the past, Lord Stride. Not when the future looks so terribly different."

There was nothing he could say to dispute her words. There was nothing he could say that would make it better, nothing he could do that would make her circumstances any different, he told himself. He was a rake, a profligate, unable to even fulfill his own life path. He couldn't change hers as much as he wanted to. All he could do was kiss the miserable look off her face, and so he did. Her lips were soft and yielded easily to his mouth, and he swallowed the sound of her choked sob when it escaped her, sucking up her sorrow, easing her burden, at least for a little while.

Her hands were tight in his hair, nails scoring his scalp and around the base of his horns, and it was too easy to scoop her into his arms. She put up no resistance, clinging to his neck as he carried her to the chaise on the other end of the room. Unlike the handful of other times he had kissed her, she was a fully active participant just then. No longer timid, shy violet shrinking from his touch, she pulled his hair and scratched his skin, her small teeth glancing off his fangs. Lips and tongue and breath, her head dropping back as his mouth moved over her jaw, her hands tightening around him as he laid her down, his body overtop hers, wings covering them like a great black canopy. There was nothing he could do to keep her from being so upset, but he could take her mind off it with this, and he had never wanted anyone as much as he wanted her at that moment.

"Let me have you, little moth."

The sensation of her nails dragging down his back was blunted by the fabric of his coat, and suddenly the layers of clothing he wore – his fine linen shirt, beautifully brocade waistcoat, his velveteen flocked cutaway tailcoat — were too much. He wanted to take her to his bed, strip her bare, and feel her soft skin pressed to his for the fleeting few hours when his skin would be as receptive before he turned to hard, unyielding marble. He wanted to stretch her legs open for him, bury himself within her plush heat, and inhale the sweet smell of her until he had made her scream, spending himself within her. *Madness.*

"Is-is it going to hurt? It is, isn't it?"

She keened again as he sucked the pulse point in her throat, letting his fangs graze her tender skin. "I shall do my best, little moth, to make sure you enjoy every moment. Remember, the skilled butterfly has no need to injure the flower."

A sharp intake of breath beneath him, another hard kiss, her hands mussing his cravat to search for his skin. "Then have me, Lord Stride."

The journey from the conservatory to his bed had never seemed farther. Gargoyles were capable of flying great distances once they were already airborne and after they'd had a full day of sun, but he could not simply launch himself into the sky like a damnable bird. They needed to catch the wind, needed to jump and let their wings lift on the downdraft, and so it was with that in mind that he turned out the conservatory doors into the courtyard, Eleanor Eastwick aloft in his arms. She clung to his neck as he ascended the steps that led to the second-floor garden, her face to his chest as he turned to the balcony, and her scream ringing in his ears when he jumped.

It was a dangerously short distance, and he'd broken many bones in his youth learning that lesson, but Silas wasn't worried. Cadmus had always been the one to instigate such experimentation, being unable to fly himself, and as a result of always bucking under the pressure of his older brothers cajoling, Silas had learned exactly how he needed to lift his wings, how to elongate and arch his body, how to catch the wind. And failing that, he had learned how to fall with the least amount of corporeal damage. He would curl himself around Eleanor and shield her from any harm, absorbing the full impact if necessary. He would heal in the sun, no matter how broken he might be, and everything would be fine. Another scream as his wings caught the wind like great, leathery sails, pulling them up, up, up and over the house, around to the upper floor where his bedroom balcony was located, landing with a soft *thump.*

Her dress came off ludicrously easy in his hands, her stays, chemise, and petticoat all quickly following. He left on her stockings, for they were tied with satin garters in a shade of bright yellow, like lemons. It seemed such a soft, personal affectation, a nod to her actual style and preference, and he realized for the first time that her unattractive wardrobe was likely not one of her choosing. Those sunny yellow ribbons were, though, and so those he left in place.

His heart tripped again at the sight of her in his giant bed – smaller and more vulnerable than he'd expected, lip caught between her teeth, her eyes wide and expectant. Soft, rounded hips, her legs pressed together to shield the thatch of dark hair between them. Her breasts were full and heavy, each capped in fawn-colored nipples that he already knew were incredibly sensitive to the stroke of his tongue. He wasn't sure he had ever had a naked woman in his bed before, not one that he'd undressed himself, at least, not that he could remember. Naked women were common enough, but after enough drink, it was impossible to tell who had stripped who, and he was just as likely to simply raise their skirts than remove their many layers.

She shivered when he lifted her foot, kneeling on the bed as he raised it to his mouth, pressing a kiss to the inside of her ankle. Silas had no idea what sort of lord she would marry, he considered as he kissed her legs, her soft kitten mewls reverberating down his stiffened cock. He didn't know if her future husband would be sadistic or cruel, if he would have strange desires that she could not fulfill, or if he would take simple pleasure in her body the way Silas himself did, and he didn't wish to dwell on contemplations of it. Tonight she would be his, and that would be enough.

She was hardly breathing as he kissed the crease of her inner thigh, a breath away from her heavenly center, and he could wait no longer. He had never been very patient, one of the many virtues he lacked, and this was a feast he had long hungered for. Her eyes had been squeezed tightly shut up until that point, but as he pushed her legs open, revealing the silky interior of the glistening petals of her sex to him, they popped open, wide and panicked.

Silas kept his gaze on her as he stroked her with his tongue for the first time — a long, slow lick from her slick core to the hooded little bundle of nerves at the top of her folds — and her reaction was one he was glad he had not missed. Her eyes fluttered shut, her head tilting back and her mouth dropping open, an expression of pure pleasure completely replacing the look of sorrow she had worn just a short while earlier.

Back and forth, he stroked her with his tongue, and on the third pass, he closed his lips around that little bud, giving it a soft suckle. Eleanor's back arched, remaining rigid as he began the cycle over again, and when he sucked once more, he thought she might levitate off the bed. When she shifted, as if she sought to move out from under him, Silas laid his palm against her stomach, stilling her movement. "The flower needs only to lie back and enjoy being fed upon, Miss Eastwick. As it is, the butterfly is certainly enjoying himself. This is the sweetest nectar he can remember tasting. Unless, of course, she is displeased with the performance thus far and wishes to stop?" No sound, but a shake of her head in the negative. "Good girl. Then lie back and let me enjoy tasting this sweet pussy flower."

He began to lick her in earnest then, focusing on her soft gasps and hitching breaths, learning which movements elicited the best reaction from her and then repeating them until her hands were wrapped around his horns. A glance up between their bodies showed him how lost to the pleasure she was — eyes closed, mouth open, her hips canting against his mouth almost unconsciously. He wanted her to drench him in her sweet nectar, lubricating the way for his cock, and from the way she was bucking against him, riding his tongue, she would do so soon.

He would need to do something with his claws. Unlike some of his brethren, Silas was not a fan of keeping them hooked and sharp. They caught on everything, and he had inadvertently nicked himself on the rare occasion when they were not tended to weekly. He shuddered to think what he might do to a human's more sensitive, parchment-like skin. His claws were trimmed and filed weekly by one of his manservants, as short as he could make them, but still hideously long and brutal looking when compared to hers. He wanted to slip a finger into her, wanted to stroke her inner walls and feel her clench from within, but he would need to ensure he had taken the proper steps first. Instead, he redoubled the effort of his tongue, licking and sucking until her chalice overflowed and his face glistened.

When her control broke, at last, it was a glorious thing to behold. Her hands tightened around his horns, dragging him closer, nails scoring his scalp. Her back arched, thighs trembling around him as she shook, a high-pitched wheeze issuing from her throat. She was going to feel amazing around his cock. He could already tell. He wanted to feel her clench, squeezing his thick shaft in her honeyed confines, wanted to make her gasp and wheeze again and again until he emptied, a river of milk cutting through the honey, his knot stoppering her, trapping their essences together.

"I concede to your point, Lord Stride. Your knowledge of butterflies and flowers is without equal, I'm certain. It is a wonder the Royal gardens have not put you on a permanent retainer to oversee the health of their fields." Her voice was breathy, and she was panting as she tugged on the velveteen collar of his jacket. "But you robbed me of my modesty, my lord, and you're still entirely overdressed."

"I'm not actually certain I can get out of this alone," he mused, pulling himself to his knees and glancing over his shoulder, attempting to eye the button placket fastened around his wings.

"I nearly forgot," she laughed. "You have a dressing assistant, of course. A servant to comb your hair. A servant to cut your meat. It's a wonder you don't have a servant on hand to powder your arse, my lord."

"And how do you know I don't, Miss Eastwick? After all, we high lords of the land are very busy napping through sessions of Parliament and drinking brandy all day. When am I to find the time to fasten my own tailcoat?"

"I'm glad *you're* the one who said it, Lord Stride."

Her laughter against the back of his neck made his cock jump as she pulled herself to kneel behind him, her palms gliding down his back until they reached the fastenings beneath his wings. "I've always wondered how this worked," she murmured, a hot breath at the nape of his neck that made him shiver.

This was any other illicit affair, he would already be inside her, her skirts hiked up around her waist, his trousers open around his thighs. But not with her.

Eleanor Eastwick was far too delicate and lovely for a fast fumble in a darkened room. His waistcoat was next, followed by his shirt. He put his sapphire stickpin through the collar of her dress at the foot of the bed, picking up the whole bundle of clothing and depositing it on the sofa across the room, his snowy white cravat like a dollop of cream atop the heap.

Eleanor Eastwick's hands were a soft glide down his chest, her nails catching at his pebbled nipples, scraping over his stomach until they reached the jutting handle of his cock. He wanted to watch her expression again, wanted to see every minute change in her as she touched him, but when her hand closed over his shaft, giving him an experimental stroke, his eyes fluttered shut, and it was all he could do from moaning.

Her fingertips explored him from route to tip, cupping his heavy sac, squeezing each of his testicles until he grunted. She seemed mesmerized by the movement of his sheath, the loose membrane of skin covering his cock head moving down his entire shaft as she stroked, pulling it back to reveal his tip, already pearling for her. When she pulled his foreskin back completely, she revealed the ridge ribbing at the top of his shaft, exploring him with her fingertips until he was unable to hold in his groan of pleasure.

"It's so big," she laughed nervously, her hands making their way down the base of his cock where his knot was filling with blood. "I can hardly believe this will fit inside me."

"Humans are quite small," he chuckled, removing her hands from him and directing her to lay back on the bed. "But I assure you, it will fit. We'll go slow, as slow as you need, my lovely. And I promise you'll love the way it fills you."

She whimpered at the first press of his head to her slick center, a hitching gasp following as Silas rubbed his cock tip up and down the length of her folds, her legs jerking every time he rolled over her clit. Eleanor sucked in a sharp breath as he pressed into the mouth of her sex, so slowly he could barely tell he was moving at all.

"Do you remember what we talked about regarding asphyxiation, Miss Eastwick? Please don't forget that you need to breathe." His palm pressed to her lower belly as his thumb began to circle over that swollen little pearl, tickling her clit as her cunt swallowed his cock. She winced, and Silas quickly bent to press a kiss to her forehead. "Just breathe, my little moth. It'll only hurt for a moment. Refind your pleasure, lovely."

The first drawback of his hips happened in slow motion. A small thrust of his hips and his thumb circling her clit, and on the third half thrust into her, she wheezed. "Starting to enjoy yourself, Miss Eastwick? I assure you, my dear, this is only the beginning." When he slid his palms beneath the rounded globe of her bottom, lifting her slightly and angling her hips, her reaction was immediate. A sharp gasp, her hands scrabbling at his shoulders, simultaneously pushing him away in tugging him closer, scratching at the back of his neck. Another thrust, this one seating him deeper within her, and she cried out. "There we are, lovely. See, that didn't hurt too terribly, did it? I'm going to fuck you now, Miss Eastwick. Your cunt already feels delicious around my cock, but I want to feel her squeeze."

She was just as reactionary as he fucked her as she was when he kissed her. Pulling his hair, gripping his horns, nails scraping down his back until they reached his wings. She was so small and soft beneath him, he barely needed to exert any effort pumping into her. His knot kissed the mouth of her sex on every thrust of his hips, and the tight, sucking sensation of her cunt was more than he could bear for long. Her inner muscles were gripping him like a vice, crying out on every backstroke as those ribbed ridges in his shaft dragged along her inner walls.

"This is the sweetest, tightest little pussy I've ever had, Miss Eastwick. Do you like the way my cock feels inside you? Because I am very much enjoying the way your delicious little cunt is squeezing me."

She whined against him when he slid a hand between their bodies to roll his thumb over her clit once more. He wanted to feel her clench around him, wanted her to milk his cock until his balls were dry, sending him into the sunlight heavy and sated; a good day's sleep for a change. He felt the jerk in her legs first, her thighs squeezing around his hips, feet kicking out, a shutter moving through her before her pussy spasmed in her throat opened, a glorious golden tone, singing for him after all. Each contraction of her muscles surrounded his cock, jerking him until his eyes rolled back, the rhythm of his hips stuttering, balls tightening and raising close to his body, and all too soon, it was all too much.

Silas surged forward with a moan, his knot breaching her, popping into place as the first contractions of his own orgasm rippled through him. She had still been clenching him tightly when he had filled her, and now she clenched around his knot, a bliss unlike anything he had ever known. He ought to have been more concerned with her welfare. He ought to have been checking in and making sure she was all right, he told himself, that the sound that ripped from her throat was one of pleasure and not one of pain, but he was lost. His great black wings beat the air above the bed as his balls pulsed, knot throbbing, his cock pumping spurt after spurt of his hot seed into her.

When it was finished, Silas was dizzy. He had never knotted a woman before, and the realization that he had now done so would likely be a mad panic in a few hours, but right now, he only felt drunk and heavy, surrounded by her warmth and her soft smell, and he sank into her, a small part of him hoping that he never resurfaced.

"Why didn't you sing at the opera? Did the crown's facilities not please the diva?"

Her smile against him was soft, and her eyes remained closed. They were still locked together, the swelling in his knot keeping them tied, and that, too, was a brand-new sensation. Her nose pressed to his chest, rubbing side to side, nuzzling against him before she answered.

"I don't care for opera, actually."

"Miss Eastwick, I demand you be sensible."

Eleanor laughed against his chest, her breath hot, her small nails scraping against his skin. "I'm sorry! I don't, though. I never have. I always preferred lieder and chanson."

"Dare I ask why?"

Her nails skated down his chest to his stomach, scratching softly. His lungs were in danger of turning themselves inside out. He was one of London's most notorious rakes, and this sort of soft intimacy was far outside his wheelhouse.

"It's someone else's words. Opera, I mean. You're playing a character. I have to feel what the character is feeling. With art songs, *I* get to feel. I get to interpret what the composer may have meant. You don't have that sort of latitude in opera. Your director is going to have very specific ideas, and the actress needs to follow her directions. I know it seems silly, but —"

"It doesn't seem silly to me," he interrupted, quickly voicing his agreement. "I remember that night I heard you perform, Miss Eastwick. There wasn't a dry eye in the house."

She turned her face to his chest, and he felt the dampness of her tears. *And you're right back to where you started, you blithering idiot.* Unlike earlier, she lays her small fingers with his longer ones, locking their hands together as she rubbed her cheek to his chest, stretching like a cat against him.

"I should be getting home soon. It's probably very late. Sometimes my sister wakes up at night, and she'll be upset if I'm not home yet."

He couldn't remember the last time he left the house in only his shirt and tailcoat, leaving waistcoat and cravat behind, but she was right. It was very late, and it was his fault that she was still in the house at this hour. He would see her home himself rather than waking Kestin's sleeping sister.

"Thank you for the instruction on the delicate relationship between flowers and butterflies, Lord Stride."

Her voice was soft, but in it, there was a smile mirroring the small upturn of her mouth as his carriage pulled to a stop before the Eastwick's home.

"I do hope you found it to be an enjoyable lesson, my dear. I take full responsibility for any ill effects you are feeling."

The smile remained on her face as she shook her head no as he raised her hand to his lips. "Not at all, my lord. No pain and no regrets."

By the time he was home, Silas felt a bit ill with himself. He hadn't wanted to let her out of his carriage, and that in and of itself was a ghastly mistake, a portent of ill luck on the air, a tightening at his throat. That shift in his chest again as he looked over the bed where she had rested against him, where she had nearly fallen asleep, where he would have been content to let her stay for the rest of her days, wrapped in his arms, tucked against him.

Silas began to pace. Eleanor Eastwick was going to be going off to marry another man. That was the plan, and it was the right thing for her to do. Why then, he thought to himself in aggravation, did the thought leave him so unsettled? He was not meant for love. He would no sooner bring children into this world, children who would only know him for a few hours a day than he would name his horse Marquis in his place. He would not take a wife and leave her vulnerable to a cruel and conniving society. Fortune seekers abounded, and every other person he knew was a vagabond in their soul. He knew too well the faithlessness of noble wives, and the thought of another man — a man like *him!* – fucking the woman he loved every day as he sat there, a worthless slab of stone, was too horrifying to even consider.

His plan was a good one. He had long considered his options, marshalled his resources, and thought through the ramifications of his actions. Maris would make a formidable Marchioness. Her children would carry on the Stride bloodline, inheriting Basingstone, the title, the lands, all of it. He'd already found a gargoyle in the far north, on some tiny frozen island, who was ready to end his time on this plane of existence. He bore enough passing resemblance to Silas that they could make it look believable. A tumble from the rooftop, shatter of marble. His sister would mourn, but then she would do her duty to the family, as she always had. Cadmus would be expecting him, and the Marquis of Basing-stone would be no more. He had thought through his plan a hundred different times a week, in a hundred different ways, and it had always seemed like the best and only option. He hated that there was doubt niggling at the back of his mind now.

You don't need to sit here feeling sorry for yourself. She's just another pretty, untitled woman, and you've had plenty of chits just like her in the past. You're not beholden to any-one. There was a pleasure house nearby, one he had vis-ited before. It was not a brothel, but a true den of dere-liction, a house where landed gentry and titled nobles alike came to slake their thirst for depravity in a shared space with each other. No names, no judgment, just mindless fucking, which was all he needed right now was to wipe his mind of the unacceptable softness the assignation with her had brought about. *And if you leave quickly, you won't give yourself an opportunity to change your mind.*

It did not take him long to arrive at the white-gabled home. Inside, there was a sea of flesh, bodies writhing everywhere he turned. A young woman he knew to be the daughter of a baronet was on her knees before a thick-set orc, a line of drool connecting her mouth to the tip of his cock every time he pulled out to give her a breath, while behind her, a human looking man pumped away, eyes squeezed shut.

There was little challenge in finding a partner who appealed to his sensibilities. Silas moved the woman's hand over the bulge of his clothed erection, pushing her fingers in a way that made the movement feel clumsy and unpracticed, the way *hers* had felt, but as soon as he let go of her wrist, the stranger's grip was sure and proficient, her hand tight as she undid the front of his trousers, drawing his stiffened shaft out.

She suckled on his cock tip and squeezed his knot, her hands moving one over the other, from root to tip. It was pleasurable, but it wasn't at all what he wanted. She squeezed his sac and massaged his knot as she took his cock down her throat, his fingers tight in her hair and his wings stretching open, but it wasn't what he wanted. He came with a choked groan, balls tight and knot pulsing, but it wasn't at *all* what he wanted. Normally, he would have stayed for another hour or two after his first spill, enjoying himself with a bevy of beautiful women of various species, but that night he only felt numb and quickly took his leave.

Once home, Silas returned to the empty bedroom they had occupied, staring at the rumpled coverlet, his nose still able to pick out a soft whisper of lilac in the air. The scream that ripped from his throat was primal, the closest he had ever sounded to his nearly feral ancestors, and the credenza to his right paid the price for his sudden, incomprehensible rage. The fine wood splintered against the wall where he flung it, the chaise following it.

He needed to get out, to get away, to see the sky and the moon and breathe the icy night air, needed to get *away* from the feeling that was clawing at his chest. He would return to Basingstone. It was too late to reach the manor that night, but if he took wing and did not wait for his carriage and horses, he could cover a good bit of ground before dawn. He would ensure he was safely tucked away on some village church rooftop before daybreak and then complete the journey the following evening.

He would leave that night, leave right now, and put this evening behind him, this evening and the way she'd felt in his arms, the unrestrained sound of her laughter, and the maddening, intoxicating smell of her far behind him. Back to Basingstone, where Eleanor Eastwick was unable to follow.

"And if I have to hear one more bloody word about it, I'll set fire to the whole thrice-damned countryside myself!" His shout rattled the windows in their casements, making the candles at the edge of the room waver. Silas paced behind his desk, fury and aggravation practically radiating out of his long, pointed ears. "Do I make myself clear, Kestin?"

Before him, the mothman stood unaffected. Bored, even. Silas flared his nostrils and gnashed his teeth, fists balled at his sides, but his steward only sniffed.

"Crystal clear, my lord."

His fingers trembled at the brandy decanter once the steward had taken his leave. A cut crystal glass, three fingers of the amber liquid, a memory flash of the port he'd shared in her shabby but cozy library. He made a noise of frustration in his throat, furious at the unloyal treachery of his own mind. Silas had been tense and on edge since he'd arrived a day earlier, snapping at anyone unlucky enough to cross his path, and Eleanor Eastwick was solely to blame.

He didn't know what he'd been thinking, saying yes to this mad plan in the first place. He was not a matchmaker, was no marriage broker. Marriage was the last thing in the world he wanted. What would he even know about the bloody subject?! Efraim Ellingboe had placed his trust in the wrong gargoyle, and it would have been smarter to simply say no from the start. At the very least, he reminded himself, he ought to call the whole thing off with the girl before they progressed any further, as quickly as possible, let her know he'd offered as much assistance as he was able, and wish her well.

Silas had never considered himself to be possessed of an extraordinary intelligence. With each day that passed, each day that she remained in his purview, he thought, throwing back the brandy as if it were some back alley pot shop brew and not a fine varietal, the supposition became a certainty.

His skin itched, feeling snug around his bones as if he'd gone to bed wet, shrinking up in the sun. His mind was a tangled mess of frustration and desire, annoyance and irritability, and he found himself drifting from pastime to pursuit to profession with little care or cognizance of anything around him. His temper was short, his patience in short supply, and seemingly worst of all, his cock was an aching agony, stiffening in the slightest breeze every time his nose caught the scent of the freshly bloomed lilacs around the moon chapel. It made no matter how often he emptied it — jerking himself in a mad frenzy until he seized, spilling like a green boy, or else, making good use of Lady Derrybrook's firm grip and willing mouth, fucking dairymaids and a duke's daughter, trying and failing every day to purge his loins of the hot, hard desire they'd developed for Eleanor Eastwick, but it was no use. His knot pulsed in a cadence that seemed to echo her name and hers alone.

He was a fool. If he wasn't, he never would've found himself in this mess with the girl, would have never offered himself up as a toy for her to cut her teeth upon. *A bloody fool!* He was one of London's most notorious rakes, a reputation well earned, one he was proud of. He was not meant for love and would never give away his heart, but that didn't mean he needed to deny the women of the city the joy of his carnal company. Eleanor Eastwick was an impediment, one he ought to remove from his path as quickly as possible. That was the sensible thing to do.

But first, he needed to have her again. He would die if he didn't. There was no other way to free his mind from thoughts of her, no way to cool his blood and keep from wanting her. He would send for her, he decided, his blood thrumming at the thought. He would send for her, would have her come here, to Basingtone. He would have her, worship her, pleasure her until his cock was limp and satisfied, his balls drained dry, and his head free of her at last. The Monster's Ball was in two weeks. Plenty of time to wring her from his consciousness before sending her off to whatever lord she would marry.

The monstrous men in attendance would fight over her, of that head little doubt. Upon reflection, Silas wasn't sure what Efraim Ellingboe had been thinking, for certainly the earl should have known that a woman such as she — beautiful, well-mannered and grace-ful, witty and humorous — should have no problem seeking a mate, particularly at an event where the men would most certainly outnumber the women, men who were all eager and desperate to marry, particularly to small, soft, sweet-smelling human women who carried offspring across species with such ease.

Lord Ellingboe had offered Silas a ten percent retainer of her dowry, a dowry he himself was subsidizing, in exchange for his assistance in securing the marriage. Not a fortune, but neither was it a paltry sum. This was a business transaction, he reminded himself, pulling out a fresh quill. He would bring her to Basingstone, he would have her, and then he would be done with the whole messy affair. It was a foolproof course of action, he decided. Dipping his quill in a charger of ink, Silas thought for several long moments, smiling at his own brilliant plan, and began to write.

The High Tea

SOCIETY PAPERS

Dearest readers,

We've previously served up a surprisingly serene cup of reformed behavior regarding one of London's favorite rakes — reliably wicked, taking wing from bed to bed, leaving many horned husbands in his own horned wake – but as of late, those predawn dalliances have curiously died down.

As previously reported, we've spotted his carriage coming and going from an unknown London address, and our keen eyes have taken note of an escorted visitor making her presence known at this lascivious libertine's lordly London home. None were as surprised as us by this devil's domestication . . . but it seems we were premature in taking this pot from the heat.

The very same night his escorted visitor left this past week, our stony-hearted rakehell was seen leaving a house of ill repute in a state of dishabille. It seems that reformation is not in the cards for this marquis.

Lady Grey

Eleanor

The northern countryside was breathtaking this time of year, as signs of spring blossomed over every hill and dale. Lambs dotted the fields, wildflowers provided a colorful counterpoint to the unbroken greenery, and once they closed in on their destination, golden gorse lit the hills of the Irish countryside.

The noble house of Basingstone was a curiosity. Loyal to the crown, situated on the northern Irish cliffs, with the French designation of their title in use. Silas Stride's accent wasn't different from any other posh, London-based lord she'd met over the years, yet the provenance of his nobility seemed quite continental. *Who cares? He and his house have no bearing on you.*

"It was so good of the marquis to send for you, dearest," her grandmother sighed, at least the tenth time she'd made the observation since they began their journey. Eleanor wondered if sighing over the Marquis of Basingtone was an action her sister had learned from her grandmother, or her grandmother from sister — or more likely, that they'd trained themselves over the last month on the automatic response to any and all mentions of Silas Stride together. "In his own private carriage, at that! He must surely be planning his marriage proposal."

"Look there, at the side of the road," she raised a gloved hand, directing her grandmother's eye out the carriage window. "Look at how tightly they stay to the side!"

Approaching on the opposite side of the packed dirt road, a shepherd led a flock of at least seventy-five heads, tightly pressed, *bahhing* their disapproval of the lack of greenery on the dusty thorofare. A sheepdog prowled on the outer perimeter, nipping at their feet, keeping the herd in line. It was an adequate metaphor for the way she felt as of late — just an opinionless sheep being led to slaughter. Silas Stride was the shep-

herd, and the moneylenders and collectors of the outside world nipped at her heels.

Fortunately, her grandmother was forgetful and easily redirected, rather like a child. She wouldn't remember alluding to Eleanor's fictitious impending nuptials
to the Marquis of Basingstone until the next instance
of sighing over his handsomeness commenced. Eleanor
didn't bother reminding grandmother that *he* was not
the lord she was hopefully marrying. *Not if he had the last
bloody title in England.* It wouldn't make a difference, in
the end. She would come home from the Monsters Ball
with an engagement, and no one would remember who
they'd hoped the lord in question would be.

The summons had come several days after *that* night.
Her heart had been in a tumult the last time she had
left the Marquis of Basingstone's home. The carriage
curtains were drawn over the windows, shielding them
from the prying eyes of the outside world. She'd sat
on the bench beside him, most improper, with his
arm tucked around her and her head lolling against
his chest. He smelled like an expensive gentleman's
fougère, an herbaceous lavender with a dark, heady
core. It was deeply alluring, somehow both feminine

and masculine at once, even *erotic*, she thought with a blush. It made her weak, and she suspected she'd never smell lavender and rosemary ever again and *not* think of him.

He'd kissed her hand before her door, once she'd fished her key from her chatelaine, the act of having to open her own door in such a way an unbearable embarrassment in front of him, and his carriage had rocked off once the door was closed securely behind her.

There had been no sleeping after that. Her feet had carried her back and forth, back and forth, across the library for hours after she arrived home, meeting the dawn the same way he likely had, the mere thought of him causing her to melt against her pillow, forcing herself to sleep for a few hours; hours that were spent dreaming of him. Her body hummed. She had never before experienced a peak like the one she'd had against his tongue and then again with him inside her. When that fat protuberance at the base of his cock had pushed inside her, she'd seen stars. It had hurt, worse than even his cock had at first, but she had still been pulsing from her peak, and as she squeezed around the thick invasion, her breath had caught, pleasure outrunning the pain, the world going white as he groaned into her hair.

She would be attending the Monster's Ball in just a few weeks, going off to wed some stranger, but somehow her heart had gone and enamored itself with Silas Stride, the most foppish, philandering gargoyle in all of London.

That night didn't deserve any special designation in her head, not now, not anymore, but when the pristine stationery had arrived adorned with his blue seal, she had been nervous and giddy, butterflies taking up residence in her chest, squeezing out her ability to breathe, the flutter of a million tiny wings brushing her heart. He had thought of everything. His carriage would be arriving to bring her and her grandmother, along with Hettie, to Basingstone, ensuring she had an escort to preserve her reputation. Meanwhile, Lucy and Coraline would be sent north for the next month, private instruction at a finishing school for young ladies, freeing her of the worry of what to do with them when she left for the ball.

I hope you will be amenable to sending your younger sisters to the esteemed ladies at Lunaswell. I can assure you that they will receive a comprehensive education in both academics and etiquette during their time there. My own sister attended several summers at Lunaswell in our youth, and I am certain you will find no fault with their rigorous curriculum in the feminine arts.

He had a long, sloped manner of writing, each stroke of his quill like a ripple on the surface of water, and as she read his words, Eleanor tried to picture them in his drawling, icy voice. The girls would benefit from attending the school, even for just a month. She did her best at home with them, but she was no governess, and she knew their education in the fine art of being proper young ladies was lacking.

"Will we be gone for very long?" Lucy had asked with a stricken expression after Eleanor had relayed the news.

"Not too terribly long, darling," she had assured her younger sister. "I'll be completing my own finishing with the marquis, and then leaving for the ball. Arrangements will need to be made for the wedding, and then everything here will need to be packed away. This is for *you*, Lucy, both you and Coraline. We talked about this, remember? We're all going to have to move once I marry. And then you and Coraline will resume your education, and in just a few years, we'll be introducing you to London society, little sister. We want you to find a good match, do we not?"

"Do you promise?"

"Promise?" Eleanor hadn't known the nature of the promise she was meant to be making, but she wasn't prepared for her sister's tears.

"Do you promise you're not just sending us away?"

"Lucy! Darling, of course not!" She opened her arms, and her sniffling sibling threw herself into them, hot tears soaking the neckline of Eleanor's dress.

"Promise me you're not sending us away and that we're going to stay together. *Promise* me."

"Of course, I promise, darling. I would never send you away for good. Where did you get such a silly thought?!"

Lucy sniffed, hanging her head. "I heard Camilla talking about the workhouses. She said if you can't find a rich husband, Coraline might be sent to be a scullery girl in some lord's kitchen, and I-I'll have to —"

Her blood boiled. She was going to have a sternly-worded talk with the part-time cook upon her return. *You won't have need of a part-time cook when you*

return. You'll be going to live with your new husband.
The thought had made her stomach tighten, a nervous braiding owed to the fact that she knew she could not fail in this, and the simultaneous quiver at the thought of marrying some stranger and not the lord with whom she had been spending all of her time.

"Lucy, I'm *not* going to let that happen. Listen to me; this is very important." Eleanor lifted her sister's chin, forcing her to raise her tear-filled eyes. "You are not going to wind up as someone's maid. We have a good name, Lucy. A good, respected name. Everyone loved father. But that name is all we have left. It's our only card left to play. That is the whole point of the marquis's assistance. I'm going to come back from the Monster's Ball engaged to some lord, and we're all staying together, all four of us. I promise you. And in a few years, when it's your turn to debut in society, no one is going to remember these hard times."

When the gilded blue carriages arrived, Eleanor was unsurprised to find Cressida, the mothwoman, in the one taking the girls north.

"I expect my sisters will receive closer chaperoning than I have," Eleanor said in a voice that borrowed some of Silas Stride's coldness.

"Yes, miss, of course. I'll likely sleep in the carriage in the afternoons so that I'm able to watch over the young ladies all night. But if we slow or stop for *any* reason, you're to wake me at once," she directed to Lucy and Coraline. "You don't have to worry, miss. My entire family serves the marquis and his household in some capacity. We take our duties to his lordship seriously."

The carriages had followed each other out of London, and the girls had practically hung out the window waving their goodbyes when they parted at last. She'd experienced her first Highland gryphon flight once they'd reached Nottingham, the gondola strapped to the beast's belly not being terribly different from the carriage they were exiting.

"Watch your step, ladies, and welcome. My name is Hectorn, and I'll be your conductor this afternoon."

The towering orc had a gap-toothed smile and a cheerful air, and Eleanor smiled automatically at his greeting. *An orc might make a very good match.* After all, Uncle Efraim and his sons were handsome and strapping, stoic but kind, and there weren't any special ac-commodations to consider regarding their anatomy or sleeping habits. *And they're probably capable of dressing themselves.*

"The take-off is the rockiest bit, I'll give you fair warning now, but Lemuel is one of the marquis's finest gryphons. We'll be in the air as soon as you ladies get settled and then touching down in Ballymena. His lord-ship's carriage will be waiting to take you the rest of the way."

Her grandmother and Hettie whooped and squealed like schoolgirls when the gryphon bounded across the empty meadow that stretched before them, and all three women shrieked when it leapt into the sky. Once they were airborne, she was forced to admit, the ride was very smooth. It took no time at all to cross the whole of England and the narrow sea, the beast's touchdown was far more graceful than the bounding leap had been.

She had met men who were gryphon-born, with leo-nine haunches and wide, feathered wings, but this crea-ture was as tall as several of its orcish conductor, laid end-to-end. She wondered if there were women who lay with beasts like this, producing their monstrous, human-sized progeny. *Well, obviously? How else would they exist?* She wondered what the result of a human mating with a gargoyle would look like, if it was even possible for her to bear a child with horns and Silas's dragon-like wings. *Would your baby turn to stone each day?* She shook away the foolish supposition with a blush. It didn't matter. She was diligent about tracking her blood, and her last menses had been the week after the Marquis of Basingstone had first come to tea. She would be bleeding again soon, and she'd not fret until then. *And besides, if he's gotten you with child, he'll be forced to support you and you won't need to marry anyone.*

Their traveling party had stopped to take tea at a small tavern once they were back on solid ground, as the coachsmith readied their horses, and her grandmother had let out a triumphant yelp, scooping up an abandoned High Tea as they sat. She and Hettie exclaimed over the High Tea supposition that some unnamed countess had been spotted in a compromising position with some roguish baronet, and an entire section of marriage announcements, the ton's most sparkling diamonds of the season landing within their comfortable settings, just as they'd planned.

As her grandmother read aloud the story of some slithering Viscount who was embroiled in a property dispute with his former wife, Eleanor considered that it was rather lucky that the High Tea primarily focused their attention on members of the peerage and gentry. How gutting it would have been to have read of her own family's financial ruin in the gossip tattler. *Bad enough that you've begun to recognize whom they are referring to in the blind items.* She'd just picked up the column while Grandmother finished her tea, perusing the blinds when she saw it.

We've previously served up a surprisingly serene cup of reformed behavior regarding one of London's favorite rakes — reliably wicked, taking wing from bed to bed, leaving many horned husbands in his own horned wake – but as of late, those predawn dalliances have curiously died down. We've spotted his carriage coming and going from an unknown London address, and our keen eyes have taken note of an escorted visitor making her presence known at this lascivious libertine's lordly London home. None were as surprised as us by this devil's domestication . . . but it seems we were premature in taking this pot from the heat. The very same night his escorted visitor left this past week, our stony-hearted rakehell was seen leaving a house of ill repute. It seems that reformation is not in the cards for this marquis.

The High Tea had fallen from her hands.

The Marquis of Basingstone didn't give a whit about her, but she had, she was forced to admit, begun to care very deeply for him. It was ridiculous. It had been only several weeks earlier that he was sneering at her from across the tea table in her father's library, scoffing at her in his exaggerated way of speaking, rudely interrupting, and implying she was up to no good. How could she come to care for him in such a short amount of time? How could she fool herself when she knew what he was like? The marquis didn't care for anyone but himself, himself and his own lustful desires. *He's a rake. An unrepentant scoundrel and you're behaving just as foolishly as every other naïve noblewoman he's bedded.*

Eleanor felt numb. She felt hurt and humiliated, foolish for the hurt, and an extra compounding of humiliation for having felt anything at all. *Lessons, that's all it was. Of course, he agreed to help you. You were foolish enough to let him between your thighs.* She'd allowed herself the rest of the day to be upset. It hadn't *felt* like a mere lesson. Dancing with him felt like flying, kissing him felt like singing, and she had already let him take more liberties with her body than she had given to any other man in the past. *And he left to spend the night in some brothel the minute you were gone. You're a fool for thinking he felt anything but lust.*

She had spent the subsequent day of their journey to Basingstone hardening her heart. She was not finished with the marquis. She would let him have her again, she decided, let him have her every day she spent in his home, as long as she was the recipient of the pleasure he had to give. These were lessons, and she intended to learn to her best ability. *All the better to seduce your husband and put every thought of the Marquis of Basingstone behind.*

With each bucolic little village they passed, she shed another layer of her vulnerability. This was a business transaction. That was all. He was executing a favor for another titled nobleman, likely so that he would, in turn, have a favor owed, or else, he was already on the repayment end of the equation. Lord Silas Stride saw her as some tatty little plaything, a temporary diversion while he frittered away his time in London. That he could earn favor with the earl in the process was likely his sole impetus for completion. The fact that his success would be life-changing for her and her family was inconsequential to him, and that was fine. She would make him as inconsequential to her in return.

And, after all, wasn't that the point? Wasn't the entire reason for soliciting his help because he was a rake? A philanderer? The one person who could prepare her to fall in love with a stranger within a weekend, or at least learn to tolerate them well enough to win a proposal of marriage? Lovemaking without consequence, that was the name of the game. *Look how well he's done his job —* *you're half in love with him already! He's playing his part.* *Start playing yours.*

"Welcome to Basingstone, miss." The mothman who greeted them at the top of the circular carriage lane before the manor bore a striking resemblance to her permissive London chaperone, and Eleanor remembered what the mothwoman had said about her entire family being in service to the Strides. "If there's anything you ladies need in your time here, Miss Winswode will see to it."

The woman who stepped up beside him was sylvan, her warm brown skin accentuated with curling gold around her eyes and down her long, graceful fingers. "I oversee the daytime staff, miss. You ladies will have your own chambermaid, and if there's anything I can do to see to your comfort while you are a guest here, please do not hesitate to ask."

"His Lordship has already arranged for flight transport for you, Miss," the mothman went on in a bored-sounding voice. "More details will be provided once I have confirmed with our gryphon provider."

They were left alone then, Hettie already giddy over the accommodations. Eleanor lingered at the cracked open door, listening to the two servants as they departed down the hall.

"You ought to get to bed now," the sylvan woman hummed, "sleep while you can. He's been in a wretched mood since he arrived. I don't envy you lot on the night shift."

The daytime staff. The qualification of *daytime* clearly meant there was also a nighttime staff. She thought that made sense. After all, the manor itself and its grounds would need to be kept throughout the days, but the lord in residence was only awake at night and would have need of a full staff to dress him and feed him and ferry him from one illicit affair to the next. Hettie and her grandmother both announced that they were going to take short naps. Grandmother was weary from the long carriage ride, and Hettie was positively gleeful at the thought of sleeping on such a fine feather bed.

They are the worst chaperones in all of England. Hettie and her grandmother would clearly not adjust to a life nocturnal. They were not used to staying up until all hours and had never experienced stage life, one that necessitated sleeping during the day and being alive and alert after the sun went down. She would likely have no true chaperone for the duration of her time at the marquis's residence. He'd likely known that. *All the better*, she thought to herself firmly. *Fewer interruptions for when he puts his tongue between your thighs.* She was furious with him for toying with her heart, even if he hadn't meant to do so, and she couldn't promise she wasn't going to beat him with her fan the instant she saw him . . . but she intended on making him pay her back in pleasure.

Eleanor was too full of nervous energy to think about resting. She changed her dress, changed her shoes, hoped her parasol wasn't too tatty and set off. Basingstone was beautiful. Hundreds of acres of manicured gardens, fruit orchards, dense forests, and agriculture surrounded the manor, ringed in rolling green hills. She exclaimed at the sight of beautiful swans gliding across the glass-like surface of a lake, downy cygnets of smoky grey paddling furiously behind their regal-looking parents.

There was a hedge maze and meticulously maintained topiaries, great winged figures and dragons amidst curving spires of intricately cut boxwoods. She strolled through the rose garden, not yet in bloom; through the endless aisles of greenery in the glassed-in orangery, exiting on a beautiful stone terrace at the rear of the main house. There was a grape arbor and a picturesque gazebo amidst a curious garden of flowers and vines that were tightly closed. *Too early for them to bloom, no doubt.* Far beyond the back of the house, she could hear the roar of the waves crashing against the base of the cliffs. It was a stunningly beautiful home, and that wasn't even taking into consideration the loveliness of the manor house itself. The leaded glass windows cast rainbow prisms throughout every room, winking in the sunlight as she strolled up the gravel path from the rose garden. *Far nicer than he deserves.*

Inside, she found what was obviously a music room; a stunning grand piano, the centerpiece of the space, nestled into the alcove of hexagonal windows. She felt decadent sitting at the bench before the beautiful instrument, glancing guiltily up to the doorway every few moments. *They didn't tell you any room was off-limits. You don't need to sneak about.*

At the first depression of the keys, Eleanor shivered. It had been far too long since she played, even longer since she had sung, and she had a feeling her voice would be rough with lack of use. She worked through scales and arpeggios, warm-up exercises that had been drilled into her head at the conservatory, up and down, until she felt a little less out of practice. The first art song she warbled out would've had her covered in mucky tomatoes had she attempted to sing it on any Parisian stage, but by the third, she was feeling a bit like her old self.

She wondered if her new husband would care for music. Silas Stride had claimed to be a great fan of the fine arts, attending concerts and the theater and ballet, the opera, and smaller venues, like the ones she had performed in, where he had heard her sing. She could only hope that whoever he was, the new lord in her life would be similarly appreciative of the arts. She didn't know if she could bear a life without music, even though she had been preparing herself for exactly that for some time. Selling the piano that had stood in their home since she was a child had nearly broken her. Lucy had sobbed the day it was taken away, begging Eleanor not to do it . . . but it had fetched a fine price, and she had reminded herself, as tears pricked at her eyes that afternoon the previous summer, that they couldn't afford to be sentimental.

She closed her eyes, focusing on the piece she played through, every bit of fear and heartache and worry of the past several years coming out in the notes. The embarrassment of the past two weeks was the counterpoint, the grief still heavy in her heart the main melody, giving up all that she was and loved, a necessary task. When the last wavering note shivered through the room, she decided that was a fine way to say goodbye to something she loved so dearly. If her new husband did not care for music, Eleanor thought it would be better to never hear a single note of it again.

She hadn't realized how rapidly the sun had gone in as she played, the entire afternoon spent exploring the grounds and sitting at this piano, reminding herself of who she used to be. It was nearly dusk, and he would be waking. Eleanor decided it would be prudent to dress for dinner, in preparation for his arrival.

Harden your heart. Harden your heart. You're a plaything to him, don't let him be more than that to you. Basingstone Manor was massive, but as the grandfather clock in the hallway ticked down to twilight, the walls pressed in on her, choking her, and eventually, she decided the best place to wait for him would be outdoors. That pretty gazebo, she thought. The sky was a wash of violet as she flitted up the stone pathway, curving around statuary and topiaries until she reached the glass-walled enclosure. She was about to pull open the door when she noticed the pathway curving around yet another statue just ahead, continuing beyond the point she could see.

Eleanor hesitated, slowly stepping away from the gazebo, deciding to follow the path a bit further. She was unprepared for the lovely stone edifice before her a short distance later. Rounded walls like a castle turret, the smooth gray exterior was punctuated with bright bursts of color, stained glass all the way around the walls at varying intervals, all the way to the top. *A chapel?* She didn't know anything about gargoyles or their culture, and she was surprised that Silas Stride would be a chapel-going sort, but there was little doubt that was exactly what this building was. *Come back to-morrow and explore.* She'd only just turned away from the intriguing arched doorway, about to head back up her path, when an unexpected sound froze her in her steps.

Footsteps, she realized. Footsteps thudded down a circular stone staircase, coming from within the building before her. Her eyes darted around like a frightened rabbit, quickly assessing where she could go, where she could hide, wondering if she could make it back to the gazebo before they made it to the bottom of the staircase, but she miscalculated the sound of the footsteps, confusing their echo for thinking they were higher up.

As she struggled in place, frozen in indecision, he appeared. A shock of white hair tumbled into his face, sharp blue eyes narrowing at the sight of her. Recognition bloomed on his face a heartbeat later, his eyebrows shooting up as she melted in a puddle of embarrassment.

He wore a rich, royal blue Banyan, the heavy lapels embroidered in silver, the hem grazing the grass, knotted casually at the waist. He was barefoot, and his legs were bare. A slow smile spread across Silas Stride's imminently punchable face, and she realized in horror that the deep V of his collar showed off a swath of his bare, sculpted chest. The Banyan was all he wore, a single layer of luxurious fabric separating her from his bare cock, a simple tug at the tie at his waist potentially leaving him completely vulnerable to her eyes.

"Miss Eastwick. Fancy meeting you here at twilight."

Fury bloomed in her veins at the amusement laced his words. He was not the vulnerable one, she realized. She was, as always. Vulnerable to the appreciation of men like Silas Stride, arrogant lords the rest of them were beholden to. She was meant to stay calm, to remind herself that she would have the upper hand for the duration of her stay at Basingstone and that when she left, she would never need to see his smug smile again, but common sense left her in that moment, and instead, she seethed. She felt flushed, but the look she cast upon him was one of ice.

"It was good of you to provide your carriage for me, Lord Stride. I am eager to resume our lessons."

His fangs glinted in the moonlight. "As am I, Miss Eastwick."

"I am eager to resume our lessons," she pushed on, cutting him off, "for the sooner we resume them, the sooner they shall be done, and I'll be leaving for the ball to meet my new husband."

His smile faltered, a shot of victory up her spine. *Good. Let him feel the fool for a change.*

"But of course," he went on, recovering quickly. "I am sure thoughts of your upcoming matrimony were all you could think of on your journey north."

His hand dropped to her lower back as they continued up the pathway, in the direction of the house. *Steady breath. He's a scoundrel and a sneak, and we don't care about him at all.*

"Have you already dined, Miss Eastwick?"

Eleanor gave him a beatific smile. "I have not, my lord. I thought it proper to wait for you." *Don't let him think anything is wrong. Remember, you're in control.*

"Splendid, my dear. I daresay it's not too late to turn your arrival festivity into something worthwhile.

She was unsurprised when dinner led to dancing, a quartet of elegantly attired moth people setting up their instruments on the far end of the ballroom, well away from the area where they would be gliding around the floor. She noticed that most of the evening staff appeared to be moth-folk, with feathery antennae, large, graceful wings, and a trail of curious iridescent dust trailing behind many of them, quickly swept away by an exhausted-looking young girl. Eleanor wondered how many of them were related to the mothwoman from London.

Being in his arms again, her body pressed to him as they waltzed – something fluttered within her, butterfly wings once more, although she had no intention of letting them fly out of control and obliterate her good sense this time. *This* time, *she* was in control.

"After dancing at the ball, will we have the opportunity to be alone with our suitors?" She kept her voice light as possible, with a flirtatious air and coy smile, allowing his hand to slip a bit lower on her hip as they turned.

"Oh, indeed. Slipping off is de rigueur. Although, I do believe the done thing is to slip off *amidst* the dancing, actually. Hold each other close, whet the appetite, and then find a quiet corner to . . . become better acquainted with each other."

"Is that our cue to leave then, Lord Stride? To become better acquainted?"

His throat rumbled in a growl, a sound for her ears only, and as they turned around the room, at the furthest point away from the musicians, once she was confident they'd not be seen, Eleanor let a sneaky hand skate down his chest, finding the bulge at the front of his snug breeches easily, giving it a squeeze. *There's no sense in pretending there's anything left to do.*

"I do believe I've had enough dancing this evening, yes. Perhaps we can take a stroll through the gardens, Miss Eastwick. I ought to let you retire a bit early this evening. No doubt your travel was arduous, but that doesn't mean we can't enjoy each other's company a bit first. I do fear your chaperone is likely already abed."

Eleanor shrugged, giving him a practiced grin. "I suppose I'll simply have to rely on you to be a gentleman, my lord. It's a relief that we are strolling at night. One does hear such tales of butterflies dipping their tongues into every flower they find out on the lawn."

Another growl as he took her by the arm, a signal to the musicians, and then they were exiting the ballroom, moving through the conservatory and out the glass doors that led to the same stone pathway.

The gazebo was a stone and glass edifice, hexagonal in shape, the interior ringed in curving stone benches.

"I confess, my lord, I was surprised to receive your summons. You departed for Basingstone with no notice; I had assumed there must be some emergency."

"A summons? My, that does sound formal."

She cocked an eyebrow and gave him a shrug as she sat on one of the benches, arranging her skirts around her with a tight-lipped grin. "What else am I supposed to call it, Lord Stride? I received correspondence and then a carriage showed up at my door. A requisition? An edict?"

He was wearing a purple velvet coat that night, the waistcoat beneath it a rich midnight blue. His ivory buckskin breeches looked invitingly soft, begging her to reach out a hand and stroke the side of his thigh. He'd fastened his hands behind him, head bent as he paced before her. She'd never seen this restless agitation before, and was at war with herself — wanting to simultaneously exacerbate it and pull him into her arms to soothe him.

"An invitation, my dear Miss Eastwick. A *rectification*, if you will. I was called back to the manor as my darling sister was experiencing some troubling pain. Did I mention she is expecting her first child? I did not like the idea of being so far with her situation as precarious as it is, so it seemed prudent to return to Basingstone for the interim. But then how was I to complete your tutelage? Having you join me here is simply fulfilling our agreement, is it not?"

The desire to soothe him died without so much as a whimper. "I see. Well, thank you for the gracious *invitation*, my lord. So, we are at the ball, we've enjoyed dinner and dancing, we slipped outside to take the air, and now we find ourselves secluded in this picturesque tableau. What would happen now, my lord?"

His grin was lascivious. "I do believe this is the part where our earlier lesson in kissing would come in handy, Miss Eastwick."

Eleanor stiffened. She did not want to kiss him. She would not tempt herself in such a way, would not allow herself to fall under his spell once more. "All right, I missed that step. Dinner, dancing, we slipped out, and now we've kissed. What should I expect *next*?"

He abruptly spun on his heel, moving to sit beside her. "Depending on the audaciousness of your suitor, I believe this is the part where you become dessert, Miss Eastwick."

He lifted her gloved hand from the bench, stroking her satin-encased fingers, raising her knuckles to his lips. Eleanor closed her eyes. If she did not see, she would not have to think about the other times they had kissed. Over her knuckles, the top of her hand, turning her arm slowly so that he could press a hot kiss to the inside of her wrist. And then up her arm, up up to the edge of her glove, his fangs nipping at the bare skin above her elbow.

"You smell absolutely intoxicating, Miss Eastwick. Has anyone ever told you that before?" His mouth continued up her bare arm until it reached the sleeve of her dress and then over her collarbone, his tongue a hot glide against her decollete, his nose pressing into the space between her breasts and inhaling deeply. "Now, you must remember your lessons, my dear. These are not mere men. Their appetites for pleasure are far greater than what you would be used to." She held her breath as he stripped off her gloves slowly. "You will need to be an active participant in these little games."

He placed her hand on the bulge at the front of his breeches, and she was right — the buckskin was incredibly soft. As he continued to kiss over the tops of her breasts, Eleanor allowed her fingers to move over the clothed shape of him. His cock was stiff, curving upward on the right side of his trouser leg. His fat bollocks, on the other hand, were being bisected by the seam, and she massaged each side of the abused sac. She was able to trace the curve of his shaft and could feel the flare of his cock head, even through his trousers.

When he pushed her hand away for a brief moment, it was only to unfasten his buttons. It wasn't the act she'd had in mind at the start of the night, but this would do, Eleanor decided. *And no further tonight.* In the cool night air, his cock was wilder than she remembered. Black shot through in white veins, thick and straining as she closed her palm around him. As her thumb stroked the slit in his tip, pulling back his sheath to reveal the shiny-smooth head, it jerked in her hand, a mind of its own, stronger than she'd expected. It was like petting a wild animal, she thought.

"Show me how to pleasure you this way, my Lord."

Silas Stride took her hand in his own, covering it, guiding it. An unexpected detour to his lips, where he kissed her knuckles once more, and she gritted her teeth. She had no more patience for his gentle seduction. *This* would actually be time well spent, she considered, forcing their joined hands back to his cock. A useful vocation, for no matter what sort of monstrous lord she landed, he would undoubtedly enjoy her teasing and pleasuring him in such a way.

"A firm grip and a long stroke, that's what you want to remember, little moth. Your touch will be most pleasurable here" — he pulled his sheath back completely, freeing his cockhead and the thick ridges beneath it before directing her fingers to stroke against them — "at the base of the head. That's almost universally true. But as you stroke, the most comprehensive pedagogy would instruct the hand to involve the entire shaft. I enjoy a bit of pressure into the root . . ."

He groaned as her hands did exactly that, and Eleanor swallowed hard, pressing her thighs together in an effort to ignore the tingle between them.

". . . While still others prefer the pressure on the midsection. A firm grip and a long stroke is the most comprehensive form you can master." He directed her to grip his shaft, squeezing her fingers until her hold on him was firm. "Just like that. Now – stroke."

She focused on the way he felt, hot and alive beneath her palm. A core of steel ran through his shaft, and she felt it every time she squeezed. His eyes were closed, and his head tipped back, and if it weren't for the occasional grunts of pleasure, she might have thought he'd nodded off. *This rakehell was seen leaving a pleasure house . . .* Eleanor pursed her lips, remembering why she was there.

"What will I need to do differently for, say, an Orcish Lord, Lord Stride?"

His eyes had been closed, but at that, they popped open, brows drawn together in a furrow. A thrill moved through her. *Good. Remind him that this is for some other lord's benefit.*

"The exact same thing, my dear. The only time you might be venturing into situations of completely different anatomy is with your reptilian and aquatic nobility and occasionally the insectoid. Otherwise, we all have more or less the same equipment. There may be different accoutrements — some have ridges, some have frills, some have differently shaped heads, but the general shape is the same, and so, my dear, the motion is the same."

She was getting the hang of the motion, she thought. The loose sheath of skin that covered his head aided in stroking him this way, and she found that those thick ridges were just as pleasurable for him as they were within her. "And your knot, my Lord?"

He adjusted himself then, shucking the trousers a bit further down his hips until he was able to completely free both cock and balls. That fat knot at the base of his cock intrigued her still. She knew his kind were not the only ones to possess such an accessory and knew that werewolves and some shifters possessed something similar. His was the very first she had ever seen, certainly the very first she had ever touched, but her time at the stage door had not left her completely innocent.

"As I mentioned before, it is a part of our anatomy specific to breeding. If you squeeze it like this . . ." He directed her second hand to cup the apple-sized knot, using her palm to pulse him rhythmically, a growl coming from his throat. "You are obscenely good at that, my dear."

"And this is pleasurable?"

"Oh, very. Although, too much stimulation cuts the act of pleasure short. As I said, this is a breeding aid. The more you play with it, the more I want to spill myself all over those beautiful tits."

Her cheeks heated, and she resumed stroking him, using her other hand to squeeze and palpate his knot in spite of his words. "This is what I should do if my suitor is a werewolf, is it not, my Lord?"

He bit back a groan as her thumb dragged over his cock tip, not easing the pressure with which she squeezed the ever-increasingly hot bulge of flesh at his base. Another little thrill of victory as he gritted his teeth, not deigning to answer.

"You mentioned there is a difference with a serpent? What would that difference be, Lord Stride?"

He had taken her hand in his own again, forcing her to abandon the pressure on his knot, tightening both sets of fingers around his cock and increasing the speed at which she stroked his shaft.

"There are two, Miss Eastwick. Two identical cocks, although what they look like is anyone's guess. They might be smooth and pointed or textured with frills and spikes, but there are always two."

Her mouth dropped open in shock. She had not been expecting *that*, not at all. "How would one even manage that?!"

He was unable to hold in his groan then. He was leaking a clear fluid that coated her knuckles, and his turgid skin had become molten. "I suppose you'll have to take up with a serpent and find out, Miss Eastwick. I can't say that I have personal experience in that particular arena."

He was pumping her hand down hard on his shaft by then, pressing into his knot. Freeing her other hand,

Eleanor cupped his heavy ball sac, pulling and squeezing, gratified by the way he groaned again. "Miss Eastwick, you might be the innocent, but let it not be said that you don't catch on marvelously quick. Just like that, little moth. I think we've turned you into a proper little wanton already." Another groan as she squeezed his sac, his cock jerking against her palm.

His testicles, too, seemed to have a life of their own, moving in their sack of skin, pulling up tight until they resembled two plump aubergines flanking the thick club of his cock. She wanted to explore these again, she thought with another blush, allowing him to move her hands back to his cock. She was intrigued by the way they shifted and moved and wanted to catalog every tiny reaction of his foreign anatomy. *Alas, you won't be here that long, and then you're never going to see or think of his cock again.*

"You already have me ready to spill, darling. How is that possible?" He was moving his hips now, raising them to meet her hands, both of her hands around his shaft now squeezed tight within his own, his eyes closed, and his head dropped back . . .

"Still, I do wonder how different an orc would be."

His groan was strangled, his look mutinous, and she was torn between the triumph of putting that last thought in his head as he reached his completion and being fascinated with the act itself. His cock jerked against her palm, a rhythmic spasm as his creamy white seed flooded out, covering her hands. His knot was pulsing, she discovered, those fat aubergines tight to his body, his cock rearing and jerking like a dragon with every spurt. It seemed like he came an endless amount, hips jerking, his knot pulsing against her, cock letting loose a river of his spend.

When he was finished, he sagged the bench beside her. She did not know what compulsion caused her to lift her hand to her mouth and dart out her tongue like a cat with a saucer of cream, and the marquis moaned as if he were in pain at the sight.

"Miss Eastwick, if you want to taste, the next time you can drink it right from the source. I daresay seeing you with my cum smeared on your pretty lips would be the pinnacle of joy. Someone could knock me off the roof in my sleep, and I'd still die happy after that."

She blushed at the mere thought, her heart a riot within her, while next to her, Silas Stride muttered a curse, looking them over. He seemed displeased with the way the night had ended, despite the physical satisfaction he might have achieved. She was meant to feel elated, triumphant, but instead ... she felt oddly empty, her chest utterly devoid of butterflies for the first time she'd spent in his presence. He pushed his feet, pulling her along with him, holding her arms out before.

"I didn't think it was going to be such a mess," she admitted with a hollow laugh. There was a small water pump outside the door of the gazebo; he gave it several pumps to get the water flowing before thrusting her hands beneath it. She squealed at the icy cold, his big hands sloughing her fingers clean beneath the spray. When there was no evidence of what they had done left on her skin, he pulled out a handkerchief from his jacket pocket, wrapping it around her icy cold, wet hands. *Cleaned away, easily forgotten.*

"It would have been messier if we had spent a bit more time on the buildup, but lesson learned, I suppose. If you permit me a small amount of time to recover, we can retire somewhere more comfortable, and I'll pay back the favor, little moth."

This was what she was meant to want, but she suddenly felt exhausted from this charade. Eleanor wasn't sure how she was meant to keep it up for another week. "I do believe you're right, my lord. I ought to retire a bit earlier this evening. I think I'm tired from the travel."

His recovery was swift, but his spine was stiff as he offered his arm. "Yes, of course, my dear. Where are my manners? Let me escort you back to your room."

When she was snug beneath the plush feather-stuffed bedclothes, she allowed herself, at last, to take a breath. That had gone exactly as she'd hoped. She'd kept control, reminded him that his lessons would end soon and that she'd be applying her new-found knowledge on another lord who was not him, perhaps had even picked up a new skill. Silas Stride was merely an accompaniment on the road to getting what she needed, and it was good to remind him of that.

So then, why did she feel so hollow? Eleanor closed her eyes, pushing the thought away, determined to go to sleep. It was far earlier than she normally retired for the night, but she hadn't lied. She was exhausted, and the mere thought of the week before her and this continued manipulation made her head heavy. *He's the one who decided the way this would work. All you're doing is following his lead.* A fair point, a true point . . . but as she drifted towards an uneasy sleep, the thought of his furrowed brow twisted her stomach as she sunk into oblivion.

Silas

The second evening, when he woke at dusk at the top of the moon chapel, he was surprised to find her there. She was sitting a short distance away, within his line of sight, perched on the back of a nearly unrecognizable gargoyle, between him and the edge of the moon chapel. Silas thought her placement seemed deliberate.

"Miss Eastwick. Fancy meeting you here. Again." Her cheeks flushed, the same adorable little blush he had been bringing to her face since the very first night they'd met, but that evening it was hard to take pleasure in the sight.

She had pleasured him with her hands the night before, stroking his cock and squeezing his knot until he had come all over her dainty hands. She had tasted his seed, and the thought of her on her knees before him — her beautiful tits on display, her rosebud lips wrapped around his shaft, suckling his cock tip while her tongue worked over his ridges — nearly made him dizzy. It should have been an enjoyable time spent. After all, he had achieved completion, and she had learned a new skill. But throughout, she kept mentioning the other noblemen upon whose prodigious members she might lavish the same attention, and something had begun to twist in his chest. *You're in danger of apoplexy. You have been all month. You ought to see a physician and find out if there's something wrong with you.* By the time he had retreated to his study after depositing her at her door, pouring himself several fingers of brandy as he began to pace, he felt sick.

When he was agitated, he paced. It was a habit he shared with his brother, both of them learning it from their father. When they were children, Maris said she could always tell when he had done something wrong because he would pace in panic afterward, waiting to see if he would get caught. The length of his study had been insufficiently satisfying, but he'd been loath to venture anywhere else in his current state of mind and decided the best course of action for his entire household had been to contain his black mood. He hadn't stopped pacing until it was time to retake his perch at dawn, and now, the following night, she was here again, and he didn't feel any better about the situation.

"It's so peaceful up here. I can understand why you have chosen this place to rest, my lord."

Silas shrugged. It was easy to slip back into his icy, disaffected mask. Everyone wore a mask in the peerage, and it did not matter if one was a human or a member of the bête monde. Armor was a necessity. Armor around his true self, around those he held dear, armor around his heart. He didn't especially like having to don it in his own home, especially in the privacy of his perch, but he felt oddly trapped. "The moon chapel was built expressly for this purpose. It has unfettered access to the sun, what little sun we get up here, and it is secluded enough that I can rest without disturbance. Normally."

She had the grace to flush again, that delectable little lip trapping between her teeth. "My apologies, my lord. I-I didn't realize I was intruding —"

"It's all right, Miss Eastwick." His voice softened nearly without his approval, and her eyes flickered up to his. The previous evening had left him feeling discomfited, but he was willing to put it behind them both if they could get back to that place of softness they had previously enjoyed. "A gargoyle guards the privacy and safety of his perch jealously, but I don't mind you being here. Although, that is my great great uncle Aloysius you're sitting on."

Silas bit back a laugh as she leapt off the lump of stone with a yelp.

"I - I brought your clothes," she choked out once she'd recovered. "I noticed last night you only wore a Banyan and . . . I didn't realize that you slept bare, my lord. I apologize for impugning your privacy."

She was red from the top of her ears to the tip of her adorably kissable nose, and he decided to play with her a bit further. Raising his arms over his head, Silas arched his back, holding onto the top of his stone throne to stretch, wings unfurling. He had a leg over one of the throne's arms, a juvenile way to sleep, perhaps, but it was what he found comfortable. At the moment, it also came with the benefit of putting his cock on display for her eyes.

"It's quite alright, my dear. And yes, unfortunately, the act of hardening the stone is not the best for delicate fabrics. Which, again, is why most gargoyles will guard the privacy of their sleeping perch quite viciously." She was approaching him slowly, on tiptoes, until she was near enough for him to extend an arm, hooking it around her waist and pulling her to his lap. She acquiesced without protest, and he wondered if the previous night was merely a misstep for them both.

"And what would happen if someone were to take advantage of your sleeping state in a lewd way? Would you even know what was happening, my lord?" Her nails scraped at his clavicle, trailing down his chest slowly until they reached the soft shape of his cock, resting against his thigh. *It won't be soft for very long at this rate.*

"Now, *that's* an interesting question. I'll start with the second part first, I think. Would I know what was happening? Let's see . . . If I were to be taken advantage of in my vulnerable state at dawn when I only just turned?

Yes, I am quite aware then. It always takes me a bit of time to fully fall asleep. I can still feel what's happening to my body, even though I can't react. Once, a small bird had the audacity to land on my shoulder and peck at my neck as if I were a bloody tree, and I couldn't do anything about it." She giggled at the confession, taking him in hand. "Similarly, I am awake shortly before dusk on most nights. If you would have seated yourself on my lap rather than my great uncle's back, I would've felt it."

He thickened in her hand, his cock slowly growing as stiff as it had been just a short while earlier when he was encased in marble. She did not pull away when he nuzzled his nose into her hair, and his heart lifted. *A small misstep, that's all.*

"Well, apologies to great uncle," she murmured against his neck. She had begun to stroke him, utilizing her newly gained knowledge from the previous evening, and it did not take long for him to be stiff and straining, standing at attention without the aid of her hand. "You said that was the second part?"

"Yes, the first part of your question — what would happen if someone were to take lewd advantage of me. Well, as I said, Miss Eastwick — a gargoyle is quite protective over the privacy and seclusion of the place where he sleeps. It is not a secret we tend to share. If you know where a gargoyle makes his perch, it is an indication that he trusts you implicitly, in which case, your ravishment of his sleeping form would likely be most welcome. I daresay if I were to wake to find you using my body as an instrument of pleasure while I slept, I would be most pleased. As a matter-of-fact, little moth, I'm going to be rather offended now if it doesn't happen."

It did not take much maneuvering to turn her, her thighs spreading wide, straddling his hips. She whimpered when he stroked his cock head against her folds, pulling his foreskin back to press his head against her clit, back and forth, until she gasped, her fingers tightening at his sides. It was always pleasurable to spill his seed as soon as he woke. He faced the rest of his night with a clear head, a bounce in his step, and if one would poll any member of his staff, they would likely say the lord of the manor displayed a better mood, as well. He wanted to fuck her like this, right here, on his perch. The intimacy of such an action made his insides quiver. It would likely not seem significant to her, but to enjoy the carnal delights of another in the place where one slept was normally a right exclusively reserved for one's spouse. He wanted her to ride his cock, and would teach her how to roll her hips, finding pleasure for them both . . . but first, he needed to get her ready.

He had taken decisive action upon returning to Basingstone. His first two claws on both hands had been cut down to the quick, filed on a diamond stone, and gentled to a softly rounded shape. He probably looked like an idiot to some of his beastly parliamentary peers, but Silas reminded himself that if anyone questioned the odd affectation, he could assure himself and anyone listening that it was an indication he was fingering a sweet, delicate cunt regularly and if they thought it odd, it was merely their jealousy showing. Eleanor's small hands hooked behind his neck as he began to rub her pussy with his fingers. Gentle strokes up the length of each delicious fold, rolling over her clit in a way that made her gasp again. When he dipped his finger into her opening, he was unsurprised at the slickness he pulled away.

"This sweet honeypot is already overflowing for me, little moth. I want you to drench me in your nectar, do you understand?" Another dip into her, her head dropping back, giving him access to kiss the long column of her throat. Once his fingers were coated in her slick, he withdrew, returning to her clit. Silas took his time exploring which movement made her jolt against him, which angle she preferred the pressure, the speed at which his fingers needed to circle to make her pant. She was already bucking against him as if she were riding a horse, her eyes closed, the unconscious movement of her hips making her bounce on his lap.

The dress she wore that night was sage green with embroidered ribbon trim across the neckline. It was several inches too high to be fashionable, the square neckline doing nothing to accentuate her shape, gaping in the corners from the pull of her heavy breasts. If she were *his* wife, every garment she owned would be minutely tailored to her figure, each seam hand-stitched just for her, each dress selected in a color that brought out the rosiness of her cheeks and made her doe-like eyes glow, each fabric picked with its drape in mind, so that she would never need to be self-conscious again. Whichever lord married her would need to spoil her. He wondered if that was a note that could be passed along to the Monster's Ball, deciding he would check and see. In any case, the dress was an impediment to seeing her lovely breasts bounce with her movement, and he was certain had no choice but to rectify the matter immediately.

She gasped in shock when he slipped his hand into the neckline, pulling out one full breast and then the other, her head whipping around as if she expected to see the entire household staff standing behind them watching.

"No one comes up here, Miss Eastwick. They all know to stay away. We have complete privacy."

"Everyone knew but me, you mean," she murmured, biting her lip and whimpering as his fingers stroked their way back between her thighs. When he sunk one of his newly manicured digits into her heat, she sucked in a breath. When he added the second, she whined low in her throat, an adorable, alluring sound. He began to stroke her inner walls, resuming the attention on her swollen little pearl with his thumb, rubbing her clit until she began to rock against him once more.

"Does that feel good, little moth?"

Her eyes were closed, her head dropped back, her jaw slack, and her mouth open. She didn't answer but nodded her head mutely.

"Oh no, my dear, that won't do it all. Your husband will want to hear that he pleases you. I'll ask you again — does this feel good, little moth?"

"Yes," she wheezed out.

"Do you like the way I rub this sweet pussy?"

"Yes, my lord."

"Yes, what, Miss Eastwick?" She said nothing, and he slowed the movement of his thumb until she cried out.

"*Yes*, I like the way you rub me, my lord. Please don't stop."

Silas chuckled. She had maneuvered around using coarse language like a true lady, but she had rescued her effort with her request. "Miss Eastwick, you do learn *so* quickly." She was so wet that it was becoming difficult to achieve the friction he wanted on her inner walls, the sloppy squelching of his movement interrupting the sound of bullfrogs at the nearby lake. "Do you want to come, my dear? Is this pussy flower ready to give me a gush of nectar?"

She was nearly unable to answer. Her tits bounced as she bucked against him, just as flushed and lovely as he knew they would be. He wanted to suck her nipples as she rode his cock, but first, he wanted to make her sing.

"Y-yes, my lord. Please."

Please sent a thrill straight to his cock. He rather liked hearing it from her lips in such a way. "How can I deny you when you ask so sweetly, my dear," he purred against her hair, feeling her spine ripple. Silas let his thumb press a bit deeper as it worked her clit, stimulating it down to its root, fucking her with his hand, and it took little time until her composure broke. Her cunt clenched around the invasion of his fingers, a delicious preview of what she would do to his cock next, and he leaned forward to suck the hollow of her throat as she moaned, continuing to rub her clit, wringing the pleasure from her until she slumped forward against his bare chest. His hand glistened when he removed it last, her mouth hanging open in a stupor as he sucked his fingers clean, licking up every drop of her sweet honey.

"Miss Eastwick, I hope you'll join me to break my fast. Perhaps we can stroll through the moon garden this evening, and I'll show you some of the statuary Basingstone is most famous for, our ancestors who built this fortress. Tonight, I fully expect a repeat performance of that on my tongue. But first, I would be most obliged if you would bounce on my cock the same way."

The first press of his cock against the lips of her sex was always as good as the first press of his mouth to hers. Silas raised her up, rubbing his slit into her dripping folds until his head breached her with a *pop*. He fed his cock into her slowly, gently pulling her hips down until she was astride him once more.

"How does that feel, little moth?"

She had hooked her arms around his shoulders as he'd filled her, and now she clung to him. "So full," she gasped.

"It's easy to fill such a tight little pussy. Roll your hips like this, love." He directed her hips until she was doing it on her own, and his head dropped back against the carved throne. "That's right, little moth. Ride my cock like a good girl."

She cried out when he trapped her still-sensitive clit between his knuckles, locomotoring back and forth. Dipping his head, Silas sucked one of her nipples into his mouth, fulfilling the fantasy. *Sucking her tits, rubbing*

her clit, all while she rides your cock. Nothing you ever do
with anyone else will be this satisfying ever again.

The ribbed ridges on his shaft were dragging over
something within her, for Eleanor had begun to increase her speed, holding onto the back of the throne for
leverage as she bucked. Silas gripped her hips, bringing
her down firmly on his knot, an exquisite pressure that
had him groaning as she bounced.

"That's it, little moth. That's just what I need. I'm
going to fill you up." He brought her down hard on his
knot, once, twice — on the third time, his back arched
and he surged up into her, his cock erupting. She was
serpentining now, pupil outrunning teacher yet again,
twisting her hips on him as his balls pulsed and his cock
emptied, jerking and spurting within her.

"Does that feel good, my lord? Is that what you needed?"

His toes curled at her voice, crooning into his long,
pointed ear as he came. Nothing will ever be this
good again. Silas moaned her name, the sound muffled
against her skin, his heartbeat thudding against her as
finished.

By the time they were stepping through the side entrance he used when returning to the house each evening, his cock was spent and satisfied, bouncing soft against his thigh as he led her by the arm. His head was clear, there was a bounce in his step, and her head lolled against his arm. It wasn't until he was bowing to her, escorting her back to her hallway so that she could dress for their evening, that they remembered she had brought clothes to the rooftop, requested from one of the chambermaids.

Silas shrugged again, brazen in his Banyan. She was not his wife, but they were in his home, with no prying eyes to see how inappropriate the situation was. "I suppose we should try again tomorrow? I'll see you in the dining room, little moth."

A bounce in his step all the way back to his chambers, shedding his robe and flinging open the armoire. He always dressed well and was a preening peacock, according to his conservative brother, but he had the desire to look exceptionally handsome for her that night.

Last night was merely a misstep for them both. They would get back to that place of softness, he would make love to her every night she was here, and by the time he would send her off to her ball, she would be out of his system entirely. It was a perfect plan, and it was going to be a good night.

"Does your brother have plans to retire from his commission? Surely he has fulfilled his rank duty by now? Unless, of course, he has chosen this as his career?"

His brows drew together. He had no bloody idea what she was talking about. "Pardon, my dear, but . . . who's retiring from what, exactly?"

She rolled her eyes as she smiled, shaking her head as if he were absolutely incorrigible, which he was. That, too, had become a familiar gesture. "For pity's sake, you told me your brother was in the Navy! I was just wondering if —"

"Oh, he's not in the Navy. Hasn't been in years. Left as soon as our father died. As a matter of fact, I don't actually know if he completed his commission or not. Not that it matters."

Beside him, Eleanor blinked. They were strolling through the rose garden that evening, tight buds just beginning to show a hint of color behind their greenery. In another month or two would be a sweet-smelling oasis, and it saddened him to think that she would not see it in such a state.

"I-I don't think I understand. When you said you haven't seen him in years, you made it sound like . . . what is it that he does then?"

It was his turn to blink owlishly down at her. She raised an eyebrow, cocking her head expectantly, the corner of her mouth tugging into a grin. Whoever married Eleanor Eastwick would need to be prepared for her spark, for she did not back down easily, and although she was gracefully mannered, her tongue possessed a wicked barb. *She's going to wind up with some dour old curmudgeon who doesn't deserve her sparkle.* Silas chuckled uncomfortably, rubbing at the back of his neck.

"Well, that's. . . that's a bit hard to describe, actually. Do you know of — you familiar with privateers, Miss Eastwick?"

She gasped beside him, hand raising her mouth, eyes as wide as saucers. "He's a privateer?! Isn't that horridly dangerous?"

"Well, no, see, he's not actually a privateer. He is . . . keeping privateers gainfully employed, one might say?"

Silence reigned as she attempted to work out the puzzle of his words, stopping suddenly with another gasp, this time both hands rising to cover her mouth in horror. "A pirate?!" she squealed in disbelief. "But-but how?! He's the son of the lord!"

"Bastard son," Silas corrected with a shrug. "Tragic that it makes a difference, I suppose, but it does. At least in the peerage. I loved my mother deeply, but she was instrumental in ensuring that my brother had no birthright to speak of."

"But how could your father allow that?"

He shrugged again, taking up her arm so that they could resume their walk. "Men do all manner of mad things under the influence of love, Miss Eastwick. Particularly if the future of your house rests upon her shoulders."

She was quiet for a moment before another question occurred to her. "Forgive me, my lord, if this sounds terribly ignorant, but wouldn't he be very heavy for a ship to carry? What if something happened in the day, if they took on water or were attacked? He would sink to the bottom of the sea!"

His laughter bounced off the stone arches surrounding the rose garden, echoing across the topiaries. "That is a fantastically troubling thought, Miss Eastwick. I shall have to ponder over that. In any case, it's not an issue for Cadmus. His mother was human. He does not turn to stone."

Her head raised sharply, meeting his eye. "So it is possible, then, for human and gargoyle to —"

"So it is, Miss Eastwick. So it is."

"So if you were to have a child with a human" — her teeth trapped her lip for the space of a heartbeat as she gazed up at him — "they would not turn to stone? Would they inherit your title?"

Silas was concerned he was going to get a crick in his neck for the amount of shrugging he was doing that night. "Any child of mine born to my legal wife would inherit my title, regardless of the mother's species. And no, they would not turn to stone if the mother were human." He felt trapped in her gaze, a liquid, glossy prison he might normally be happy to live in, but at that moment, it felt particularly oppressive. "A true stone gargoyle requires two gargoyle parents and a very long birthing process. My sister will be hatching her egg any month now. She's as big as the moon."

Her laughter, unlike his, tinkled like a crystal bell around the open garden, golden and bright, swatting his arm with her reticule. "Oh, she is *not*, you wretched man! She's *beautiful*. I can scarcely believe that you're not twins. She said you both favor your mother . . . Wait, so she's not going to give birth to a live baby? You hatched from an *egg*?" She began to laugh again, attempting to disguise it with her gloved hand and doing a poor job. "Like a lizard?"

Silas scowled down. "No, not *like a lizard*. It is a very large egg, granted. I'm told the birthing process is horribly painful. Our mother died in childbirth from a bleed that could not be stopped. And it's less of an egg and more of . . . a membrane, I suppose. It's placed in a warm, sunny spot until it hardens to stone. Marble, in our case, obviously. My best friend, when we were children, was made of jade, a stunning green color. I was always jealous. But that is essentially our infanthood.

Once we hatch, we are self-sufficient, unlike human infants."

"I don't know if I'm fascinated or horrified," she admitted with another laugh, and this time his icy tone melted with her crystal bell, the golden tone from her throat softening his sharper edges into a beautiful melody, and a giddy warmth suffused him. "Well, I suppose if I meet a gargoyle at the ball, I won't have to worry about laying any eggs, right, my lord?"

The warm feeling faded, a cold stone turning over in his stomach. "Quite right, Miss Eastwick. And a lucky lord he would be."

It was his second favorite place in the world to be. The first place position was occupied by the space between her breasts. Her skin there was as soft as a cloud, as fragrant as lying naked with her beneath the lilac grove, which he had done, as warm as a hearth, and as comfortable as his perch. He did not know what it was to sleep in his living form, but had to imagine the soft serenity of laying his head at her breast and breathing her in was just as peaceful.

His second place in the world was where he currently was, with his head nestled betwixt her thighs and his mouth on her cunt. She was ready to come for him, he could tell by the way her thigh trembled as he licked and sucked on her clit, sweet nectar streaming from her. He loved having her this way. That swollen little pearl would throb against his tongue as she climaxed, flooding his mouth with her sweet honey until his cheeks glistened and he was replete, like the fattest, most satisfied butterfly in the field.

They had repaired to the library after dinner, as it was sheeting rain that night. She had dropped to her knees before him, asking for a lesson on pleasuring him with her mouth, and while his head had seen warning in her request, his cock had been only too happy to oblige, perking right up the instant she'd licked a tentative stripe over his head.

It seemed bizarre to him how responsive his body was to her every clumsy, unpracticed overture. He like a firm grip, a deep suck, and a good, hard fuck. He'd cultivated the skill of being an excellent lover, but what he personally needed to be satisfied was rather straightforward . . . so why, then, did he feel his balls quivering, already eager to spill at the first tentative, shallow suction of Eleanor Eatwick's lovely rosebud mouth? His knees were trembling with the effort of holding himself up as she bobbed inexpertly on his shaft, his wings spread, hips rocking ever-so-slightly, spine rippling with the need to fill her mouth.

"What will I need to do differently," she gasped, drool connecting her mouth to his glistening cockhead, "with an orc or a minotaur? Will those lords be pleased with the same technique?"

It was a wonder he hadn't lost his erection immediately. Instead, he'd hauled her up to her feet, placing her on the table and spreading her legs wide. Dropping into the chair before her, Silas ignored the question entirely as he pushed up her skirts, and focused on the way she gasped under the ministrations of his tongue. He was positive she was doing it intentionally.

She had been there for more than a week at that point, and everything was going exactly to plan. He had made love to Eleanor Eastwick nearly every day since her arrival, exactly as he had planned. Sometimes, several times a day. Her time at Basingstone was drawing to a close, which meant her time with him would be similarly ending, and every time they were together, she made a point of reminding him of the way she would be applying her lessons on someone else.

It was silly to be upset. Outrageously unfair, in fact. That was the whole point, after all, and she was *meant* to be looking ahead to her time at the ball, and the husband that would follow. It didn't make sense that every mention of another lord and the way she might pleasure them was a lance to his heart, particularly when bringing her here had been his bloody idea in the first place. At least he'd managed to turn her attention away from those unnamed and unknown lords for the moment, distracting her with the talent of his tongue, and quietly mourning that it was likely one of the last times he'd do so.

When she came, it was with a tiny mewl, the lusty moan he knew she was capable of swallowed down, as she always did when they were indoors. Outdoors she was not afraid to open her throat and shower him in the glory of her beautiful voice, but in the manor she was too embarrassed at the thought of being overheard by a servant. Her fingers wrapped around the base of his horns and her hips canted against his mouth, spreading boneless across the desk when she was finished.

He could make her come again if he acted quickly enough, he had discovered. Her clit was wonderfully sensitive and receptive, and although she shied away from any further attention from his tongue, he'd learned the pressure of his cock immediately within her and his fingers circling over her hood would have her clenching and moaning again in short order. His balls were tight and he needed to spill, and then perhaps after, she would allow him to sink into that heavenly spot between her breasts.

Silas reversed their positions, bending her over the desk. She keened when he pressed into her, his cock sliding home within her snug confines. She panted he began to pump into her, pulling her hips back to him on every thrust, and shook beneath him when he pressed his fingertips to her, beginning to circle. "Oh, it's not enough to tremble, little moth."

The hand that was not otherwise occupied at her breast gripped her leg just above the knee, pulling it a bit higher over his hip. The adjusted angle made her head fall back and her mouth drop open, a wheeze rushing from her mouth as if her lungs were the cracked bellows of an ancient organ, and Silas relished the noise.

"The sounds of your pleasure will spur your betrothed on. There's no sweeter enticement for a man than the knowledge that *he* is the one causing those sounds. Silence is for the temple and the tomb, not the bedroom. If you moan for your husband, his cock will be hard for you every waking moment of his existence."

Pressed into the juncture of her sex just above where his cock filled her, two of his knuckles trapped that little pearl of pleasure, that spot he'd said he wanted to taste with his tongue, rolling it steadily. His knuckles rolled with the same rhythm as his hips, and her back arched. Eleanor was unable to stopper the wanton moan that left her mouth, echoed by his groan at her neck.

"That's it, lovely. I want to feel your heat squeeze me tight. Now . . . let me hear you sing." He increased the tempo of his hips, snapping against her, his knot threatening to breach her on every thrust.

When she clenched around him, her hitching gasps had opened to high-pitched moans, each one punctuating the slap of his balls against her. His spine quivered and his cock jerked, knot throbbing at the lips of her sex as he spurted into her. He'd made the mistake of knotting her already, and although it was the most pleasurable sensation he'd ever known, Silas knew it was unwise, and endeavored to control himself as best he could. When he turned her to face him, he leaned in to claim her lips, soft and sweet, wanting to sink into her warmth. Eleanor turned her head, and his mouth grazed her hair instead.

He could tell himself a pretty lie, that she'd simply not anticipated his kiss and moved unthinkingly, but his heart knew it was intentional. It was the first evening since she'd been in residence that he sought to be free of her company. When she made to follow him down the corridor once their clothes were righted, he stopped her.

"Would you like me to escort you back to your chambers, Miss Eastwick? Or are you capable of managing on your own?"

"Oh. I-I thought we might —"

"I have work to attend to, my dear."

She shrunk at his sharp tone, and he wanted to bite off his cruel tongue. "Yes. Of course, my lord. I'm quite capable of managing on my own."

When he stalked out of the house shortly before dawn, it was still raining. She was waiting for him at the side door of the conservatory to walk with him to his perch, as she had done every morning since the first one he'd found her on the moon chapel's roof, with an oiled silk umbrella, wearing her pelisse.

"There's no sense in you getting wet, Miss Eastwick. I'll bid you good day."

He wanted her with him. He wanted to hold her and have her and love her, but she was going to be leaving that week to marry another. He knew he ought to not take his mood out on her, but he was heavy and sad, and the realization, as he walked, that every blade of grass and fragrant flower at his home would now forever remind her of him only compounded his sadness. Every room of his house would smell like her, every shine of the moon upon the lake would mirror the luminous shine of her eyes. He would need to put his plan into effect as soon as she left, he realized, for he could not stay here when she was absent.

The rain was still torrenting down and he'd only just hardened to smooth marble when he felt it. He'd not heard her following him, too wrapped up in his own melancholy to have heard anything, but he felt her hands on his face. It was impossible to differentiate between her tears and gusting rain, but he felt the shudder of her sobs as she pressed her forehead to his. Her soft lips against his unyielding ones, once, twice, three times as her shoulder shook. He wanted to be able to pull her into his arms, to hold her tightly to him and never yield her to another, wanted to tell her loved her . . . but he could not. She was a creature of the daytime world, and he was a worthless slab of stone.

His sister was already in his study when he pulled the door open, bringing Silas up short. Maris didn't even bother glancing up from the blotter, her quill moving swiftly across the foolscap. When she finished, she scooped the paper up quickly, waving it back and forth to dry the ink in a hurry.

Two can play at that game, darling sister. He pushed past her, moving behind his desk with his nose in the air. Silas kept the silence as he poured himself a glass of the floral ratafia that had been brewed up for his guests. Much like the rainbow prisms cast by the sun across the floors and those blasted swans, Eleanor's sweet grandmother and her nurse were creatures of the daytime, and they concerned him very little, although he was gratified to hear that the two were clearly enjoying their time in his home. Ratafia was not his preferred drink of choice, but Celestia had made this batch with a healthy slug of steam-distilled violets and lilac, along with a goodly bit of fine gin, and the heady whiff he got from every sip made his cock jerk against his thigh.

Maris rose from the desk imperiously. As her pregnancy progressed, she'd taken to dressing in the style of the deposed French court, like bloody royalty. He'd reminded her of what had happened to that queen, to which she merely rolled her eyes. Crossing the room, she poured herself a finger of the fragrant spirit.

"How exactly is it that you know Miss Eastwick, brother?"

"Do you really think you ought to be drinking that? I thought the accoucheur said nothing too stimulating?"

She waved her hand. "I'm not using that silly man. I've already sent him away. Until an accoucheur gives birth, I'll not be hearing birthing lectures from any of them. A midwife was good enough for all the Strides who came before us, and that's good enough for me. Perhaps I don't mean to drink it at all. I was considering just sniffing it, the way you are. Don't change the subject."

He grit his teeth. "I am assisting her on behalf of Efraim Ellingboe. The earl contacted me many weeks ago, asking for my consultation in the matter of his near ward's marriage prospects."

"You know, it would be nice if you were to take as much interest in your own matrimonial future as you are for a stranger."

"Lord Ellingboe is no stranger," Silas snapped back. "The girl is charming and beautiful, and it was my duty as a gentleman to assist her in her aim."

"Her aim," Maris echoed, sniffing at her drink. "And what of your aim, brother? You know, I heard that Dame Marencragg is going to be visiting her youngest daughter in the highlands next month. It would be fortuitous to set up a —"

"No."

"You're not even —"

"I said *no*, Maris!" His voice rumbled like a thunderclap, a tone he very rarely had needed to use and certainly never against his sweet baby sister. "I am not going to treat with another gargoyle clan. Get that out of your head. That only leads one way, Maris. There is only one ending to that scenario. I will not be the first Stride Marquis to *not* hold the front. I will not acquiesce a single pebble of land that our great-grandfather fought for. Fortune seekers and land barons, that's all they are. Basingstone is home to more moth-folk than any other principality in the northlands. Do you have plans to rehome them all when you give up our birthright? Stop bringing it up because it's not going to happen as long as I have breath in my lungs. If you want to be Marchioness so badly and acquiesce all that we hold the instant you wear the title, be my guest. You know where I sleep. Push me off the roof and have done with it, sweet sister."

Across the table, his sister merely cocked an eyebrow. "Is this Miss Eastwick not a fortune seeker?"

"She is not," he replied hotly. It didn't matter if she had run warm and cold for the past week with him; it didn't matter how often she brought up the other lords she might meet and marry. After all, that was what she was meant to be thinking of. Any feelings he had developed along the way were not her concern. Still, he would not sit idly by and allow her good name to be slandered, particularly under his own roof. "She is a charming young woman, vivacious and intelligent and extraordinarily talented. She's looking for a husband, not a gold mine. She seeks to ensure her family's security. Isn't that the whole point of marriage?"

Silas felt hot; his collar suddenly unbearably tight. His cravat had turned into a noose, and his hands clutched at the desk, shaking with the effort to keep from pushing himself into a standing position and begin pacing about the room like a tiger. Across the desk, Maris looked entirely calm.

"You're right, of course. I certainly cannot blame Miss Eastwick for wanting to secure her family's future. Fate deals a heavy hand to the eldest daughter, always," Maris sniffed. "I suppose I ought not to be surprised. You have always had a predilection for humans."

"A *preference*, sister. A preference does not a predilection make. And are you now passing judgment on such matters? I was under the impression your only concern was seeing me married, to whom didn't matter."

"You're right about that, Silas," she sighed heavily. "I'd be satisfied to see you marry the teapot at this point. In any case, it doesn't make a difference. The girl clearly has no love for you."

He stiffened, wings rustling in annoyance. "What is that supposed to mean?"

"It means she can barely stand the sight of you. I daresay your reputation likely preceded you, brother. To your own point, this young woman is looking for a suitable match, sacrificing her freedom to lift her family into a better social stratum, just as a good daughter ought to; goddess knows it's the only thing marriage is good for. She's probably eager for you to keep your distance, rather than tainting her reputation by proximity. She is a respectable young woman, and she's looking for a respectable gentleman, not one who puts a blight on his family name every time he opens his bloody trousers. A shame there's something clearly wrong with her."

At that, he could not help himself. He was on his feet before sense could prevail, launching himself across the room, hands clenched at his sides. "What kind of asinine declaration is that? Nothing is wrong with her! Why would you even say that?"

"She's not going to the Monster's Ball for no reason, Silas, for pity's sake. There must be something —"

"Human men have no appreciation for the rarity of a woman like that," he sneered. "She is beautiful and charming and witty and —"

"And talented, yes, you mentioned. Don't forget vivacious. I believe you called her kind and gentle-hearted just yesterday. So I suppose my only question, dear brother, is why are *you* not marrying the girl? You're quite obviously in love with her."

Silas stopped short. The room was spinning. What the bloody fuck is in that ratafia? The walls were shrinking around him, and the shape of his sister seemed to grow in proportion. "I-I'm not . . . don't be ridiculous —"

"Silas," she sighed, "it couldn't be more bloody obvious if you wore a sign painted around your neck."

"It doesn't matter." His voice was a low murmur, and suddenly, he was exhausted. "She's gone. She's going to the Monster's Ball, and then she'll be married to another."

"So stop her. She's not there yet, you dolt. I don't see why you won't just —"

"Because it's not fair," he shouted again, his voice ringing through the rafters. "To take a wife of another species would mean to be absent from her life for half of it, Maris. What is the sense of having a partner that you love only to leave them vulnerable to a cruel world? Am I to make my wife sleep throughout the day and wake at eventide with me? Am I to make her shun her friends and family to exist at night with me and me alone? I can't. I won't. I won't ask that of her, and I can't bear to know that she's living a life that doesn't include me in it."

His sister rubbed at her eye, a thoroughly aggravated move. "Silas, listen to yourself. The girl's been here for two bloody weeks. Celestia said you're together every night, and apparently, you've been spending all of your time together for the last month. Her family is clearly used to it. What friends are you speaking of? The ones who've assisted since her family's downfall? Because it doesn't seem like she actually has many of those. She stays abed every day past noon. Kestin said she goes to the moon temple each evening and waits for you to wake. That doesn't sound like someone who's making some arduous sacrifice. Now if you truly have no intention of seeing the responsibility to your title through and want to run off and play pirates with our brother, then I suggest you hurry up and leave. I'll miss you every single day, but I can't bear to watch you make yourself miserable and ruin our family name in the pursuit of your misery. I don't especially *want* to be marchioness, Silas, but mercy knows someone needs to be accountable for the Stride name."

He was going to combust. Silas raised a shaking finger, jabbing it in his sister's direction. "How do you know about that? What sneaking, blabbing *rat* bastard told you that?"

She rolled her eyes again. "Oh, please. It's all well and good that you hand-picked Luenn to be your confident as well as brother-in-law, Silas, but if you truly expected him to keep all of your secrets, then *you* ought to be the one sucking his cock, brother. He's a rat bastard of your own choosing, but he's trained up remarkably well. *Stop* changing the subject. What are you going to do about Miss Eastwick?"

He was sinking into a sea of stupidity, one of his own making. He was trapped in the hull of the ship, a worthless slab of stone, and there was nothing he could do. He'd sent her off to another's arms instead of holding her in his own forever.

"It's too late," he whispered brokenly. "She's already gone."

"For pity's sake, do I have to *fucking* do everything?!" Maris pushed to her feet, flinging the glass of ratafia into the fire, and the flames surged. "Go pack a bag right now, you *fucking child*, and go after her. You have an invitation to the ball, Silas. Go claim your bride. And I swear to the moon, if you bollocks this up, I *will* push you from the roof. You're too stupid to wear the title. I'm going to the gryphonrie to have one of the males saddled. They can carry your weight. As soon as dusk falls, you get there, and you *claim* her."

She was right. There was no way to go back to his prior lifestyle, not now. He'd already seen that. There would never be another for him, and empty sex with an endless succession of nameless women would never fill the hole in his heart, shaped like her name. *Eleanor Stride, Marchioness of Basingstone.* It wasn't too late. It couldn't be too late. He wouldn't let it be. There was only one reason the titled lords of the bête monde attended the Monster's Ball, and this year, he would be one of them. Maris was right. It was time to go and claim his bride.

Eleanor

B roadstone Hall sat atop the cliffside in Maidenbury, overlooking the crashing waves much in the
same way Basingstone did on the opposite coast.

The manor itself was a formidable thing. Silas Stride's
home was impressive and beautiful — picturesque and
gleaming amidst the rolling greenery of the northern
countryside, stately and airy, far too nice for a scoundrel
like him, but Broadstone was *massive*. Eleanor was
grateful for the concealment of her carriage as she
gaped through the lace-covered window, taking it all in.
With high stone walls, peaked towers, and turrets, the
architecture was gothic and imposing, and home for the
next several days.

As the carriage navigated up the private road, she spied a massive expanse of gardens and pavilions, stone paths intersected with statuary and archways, topiaries and fountains, and outbuildings as far as the eye could see. Spires sliced through the grey Dorset sky, and at the roofline, the black silhouette of gargoyles squatted. Eleanor shivered. It was hard to believe she'd been clear across the country just a short while ago.

"Is it able to fly that far, truly?" she had asked him shortly before dawn. "It's not going to get tired and drop out of the sky like a stone?" The gryphon that was being saddled for the journey had given her a swift, sharp-eyed look over its leonine shoulder, and she blanched. "Can it understand me?!" she hissed to the marquis, balling her fists at his arrogant chuckle.

"Well, I should certainly hope so, my dear," he drawled. "Elswise, how do you expect her to follow the directions she's given? They have to know the destination in order to deliver you there, of course. It's not magic." She glared up, but he took no notice. "And besides, gryphons are some of the most intelligent creatures in existence. I've no doubt that if they possessed hands and a quill, they would be able to sit and write the most divine of poetry and work out the most complicated of mathematical equations. Gryphon gondola is a perfectly safe way to travel, Miss Eastwick, probably more so than a carriage. There's no need to fret."

"This is a female?" She could see plainly that it was, as soon as the question was out. The creature that had taken them from Nottinghamshire to Ballymena had been thicker set, heavier with muscle, possessing an enormous pair of fat, fuzzy bollocks the same size and dark brown color of a wagon wheel.

"This is Myla. She's our beauty, but aside from being stunning to look upon, she's also the most agile flier in the nest. I assure you, Miss Eastwick, you have nothing to worry about. She'll be able to deliver you to Sherborne in one piece. From there, it's only a short carriage ride to Dorset and your destiny. Someone will be waiting to collect you."

He'd bowed before her then, holding his hand out for hers for a yawning moment before she complied, realizing what this was.

"I wish you good fortune at the ball, Miss Eastwick." He'd hesitated then, and her eyes had followed the bob in his throat as he swallowed heavily. "I shall look back on our time together . . . very fondly, my dear."

Goodbye. Even though she had spent the last week hardening her heart against him, saying goodbye had somehow not figured into her planning. She had imagined herself beneath Silas Stride, had reminded herself that he was a cad and meant nothing to her, as she meant nothing to him, and had envisioned herself at the ball, attempting to catch the eye of some orcish lord, perhaps . . . but the interim, getting from point A to point B had never crossed her mind. Her face heated, alone on the stage, fraught with the expectation of what would come next.

"I thank you again, Lord Stride, for your generous donation of your time and your gracious hospitality. Your instruction will be put to good use; I can promise you that. I only hope that someday, I will be able to repay you for your time."

"No repayment is necessary, my dear," he'd murmured, kissing the top of her gloved hand. "The pleasure was all mine. Bon Voyage, Miss Eastwick. I do hope you find what you're looking for."

She was glad for the dark confines of the coach as her tears overflowed once the door closed behind her, shutting out the sight of Basingstone and Silas Stride for good. When the sun broke over the horizon, only a short while after they'd been in the air, her heart shuddered. *That was that.*

The difference between the two beasts was evident once they were airborne. Myla was more graceful in her take-off, but it quickly became evident that the consequence of being lighter and more agile meant that she coasted upon the current more than Lemuel had. The small coach swayed from side to side as the gryphon rode the air current, but it likely aided her in flying longer distances as well. It seemed like no time at all before her great Eagle wings were flapping, circling Sherborne before making her descent.

Perhaps you'll make some friends, she told herself on the carriage ride to Maidenbury. *The other women in attendance are going to be in the same position as you, you're all looking to snag husbands who likely know each other. Finding allies is important.* Her time on the stage had served her just as well as her tutelage with the Marquis of Basingstone. Rivals abounded in the world of the theater, and it was important to make the right sort of friends. To a certain extent, all of the women attending the ball were vying for the same ultimate end, but according to Lord Stride, the monstrous men would vastly outnumber the women.

"There will be plenty of chaps to go around," he explained, his voice strained with the exertion of what his hips were doing down below.

Eleanor had been unable to respond at the time, with her back pressed to the wall and her arms around his neck, her legs wrapped around his narrow waist as he pumped into her. The pressure of his knot teased her every time it kissed the mouth of her opening, and the drag of the thick, ribbed ridges against her sensitive inner walls had rendered her speechless.

"You still want to employ your feminine wiles to ensnare the lord of your choosing. I know all of them, and they're all the greedy sort." His words were interrupted by a groan of pleasure, his eyes fluttering shut briefly. "That's right, little moth, squeeze my cock just like that. I have to admit, I am greatly going to miss fucking this tight little pussy flower." Another groan, his fangs dragging over her shoulder, before he continued. "None of them want to be left out of belonging. If you catch the eye of one, others will follow suit, so it's important to act early, my dear."

The world had gone white at that point, her body tightening around him, the heady, herbaceous smell of him making her dizzy as she clenched, his groan in her hair sending a ripple down her spine.

He was right, of course. She would need to make her play on the first night, advertise her eagerness to be a good wife to one of the monstrous lords in attendance, and then close the deal by the second day. She had no doubt some of the other attendees would be similarly prepared, and they would likely not all be pursuing the same nobleman. *You establish that you're not direct rivals, and then you make friends.*

All too soon, she was gaping out the window at the sight of the manor. Broadstone was similarly situated on the cliffs, and she could hear the sound of the distant waves as a footman extended a hand to assist her descent from the carriage, and her name was announced.

"Miss Eleanor Eastwick, daughter of the late Philip Exeter Eastwick, Esquire, of London." There was no turning back now.

The footmen and guards around the front of the Château were all orcs. Their hulking presence, combined with her earlier supposition that an orc might be her best bet for a match, made her stomach swoop. Broad shoulders and arms heavy with muscle, thick, tree trunk-like thighs, testing the density of their tail coats and breaches with every step they took. She couldn't deny that an orc might be intriguing . . . *their cocks are liable to be so big, they'll cleave you in two.* Her cheeks heated at the thought. Silas Stride wasn't nearly as big as an orc, and the club in his trousers had already been a bit of a squeeze.

"Welcome, Miss Eastwick, to the Monster's Ball. We are so delighted to have you as a guest at Broadstone for our festivities." The man was gimlet-eyed and copper-skinned, with a wide, beaming smile. He looked human enough standing before her, but she could tell from the silver sheen of his gaze that he was not. Much like Maris Stride, it seemed as if Master Bow had taken the Court of Versailles as his fashion inspiration for the day. He was dressed in a rainbow of pastels — a pink cutaway coat, over top a waistcoat of icy blue brocade. His cravat matched his cuffs — thick frills of lace, reminding her of the French royal palace. Eleanor could not help but return his beaming smile.

"I am Master Bow, your master of ceremonies for the weekend. I'm on hand greeting all you lovely young ladies this afternoon, but if you follow these good gentlemen inside, you'll be assisted to your room. If there is anything at all you should require, my dear, don't hesitate to make the request find its way to my ear. You have plenty of time to dress for dinner and prepare for this evening's entertainment. With a flourish, he produced a silver domino mask, his eyes shining out from behind it. "If you've not brought your own, fret not, dearest one. We have plenty of options on hand for every fair maiden in attendance."

A bal masqué! She had not attended one of the masked celebrations since her conservatory days, and the thought made her giddy. "Thank you so much for the kind welcome, my lord. I am so looking forward to all that is planned. Will we be introduced to our hostess this evening?"

"Ah, you'll be greeted as soon as you go inside, lovely girl! Countess Stalbridge is looking forward to assessing the potential of every suitor in attendance, as well as our fair diamonds. The bête monde and the ton are not as different as you might think, my dear. The same customs are observed, and the same itinerary as you would find at one of your human balls will likely be quite similar to what you will experience in your time here. Your bags will be brought to your room as you proceed to the grand foyer to be greeted by the countess. I do look forward to seeing how brightly you shine, Miss Eastwick."

It had been such a warm welcome that she couldn't help the giddy excitement she felt. She had work to do, Eleanor reminded herself. She was not here to have fun, after all . . . but it was already a far cry from the disaster at Lady Harthington's ball.

The interior of Broadstone was just as impressive as the outside. All around them on the walls were huge murals and tapestries of men and monsters, riding together, hunting together, fighting together amidst the dark paneled wood and sumptuous draperies. And there, in the middle, was the countess. Eleanor swallowed hard. She was no stranger to dowagers, but the Countess of Stalbridge had a heavy, penetrating gaze as if she could see through to Eleanor's very soul the second the woman's eyes met hers.

She was announced again, and the countess raised an eyebrow. "Miss Eastwick. We are so pleased to have you joining us. I trust your journey south was without incident?"

Eleanor curtsied, giving the countess her very best, most charming smile. "Thank you, my lady. You have such a beautiful home. I am most grateful that you have opened your heart and your doors to all of us for this ball. And yes, thank you, my travel was quite enjoyable, actually. I was just thinking that it's hard to believe I was on the other side of England just this morning. Gryphon gondola is an amazingly fast way to travel."

"Gryphon?" she mused with a raised eyebrow. The countess was a handsome woman, regal and refined, with arched eyebrows and a cat-like glare. Her copper skin glowed like a shined-up farthing, and her cheekbones were high and as formidable as the gaze she swept over the room. "I see the Marquis of Basingstone spared no expense on you, my dear. And who is the sponsor of your season, Miss Eastwick?"

Her cheeks heated at the mention of *him*, but she mentally pushed it away. *We're done with him. We're never going to think on his name again after this moment.* Eleanor knew that it was not a question the countess would likely be asking the other attendees. Normally the season was paid for by a parent or sibling, occasionally a grandparent or an aunt. Seeing as she had none of the above, it was reasonable of the countess to ask. "The Earl of Chwyllenghd, my lady, Lord Efraim Ellingboe."

The countess's arched eyebrows shot up in obvious surprise. "Efraim Ellingboe, who would have thought. It's an amazingly small world we all live in together, is it not, Miss Eastwick?"

She dipped her head respectfully. "I take it you know the earl, my lady?"

"Oh yes, I know the earl *quite* well."

Eleanor was shocked at the coy smile that curved the countess's wide mouth, her eyes sparkling. That was not the look of someone who'd met the earl once at some stuffy party. *Uncle Efraim!*

"Well, any friend to the house of Chwyllenghd is a friend of ours. I have every confidence that you will achieve what you are seeking this weekend, Miss Eastwick. I daresay you're in a better position than some of the other young ladies in attendance, but such is fortune. What you may have found lacking in the ton, I assure you, the bête monde will adequately fill in the gaps. Here is your itinerary. Please sign our registry at the end of the table there, and your ladies' maid will take you to your quarters."

There was a small queue forming behind her, she realized, as other attendees arrived. Curtseying deeply, she quickly moved down the long, formal table, finding the registration book opened and quill already set out. There was no maid immediately waiting, and she did not want to appear to be eavesdropping on the newcomers being greeted by the countess, so she took a few steps through the arched doorway, finding a beautifully and equally severely appointed parlour. Her heart was heavy, but he needed to put that behind her and focus on the future. *Everything is going to work out. And look, everyone here is so nice already.* That was, at least, until she was approached by another young woman.

"You there. Girl. I want tea delivered to my room. Something with lavender, not too stimulating, with cream and sugar. I didn't think I would need to be wondering about searching for servants this way."

Eleanor was so stunned that she glanced over her shoulder, assuming she would find the aforementioned servant hovering behind her, likely cowering from the imperious tone of the woman's voice. There was no one. There was none but the two of them in the grand parlour, which meant . . .

"How many different servants do I need to ask? I don't want to be kept waiting all day."

"Excuse me?!" Eleanor cut in, cheeks heating. "But you're very much mistaken. I'm not one of the servants. I'm a guest, like you, presumably?"

She wasn't certain what she was expecting, not after such a rude beginning to the conversation, but if it had been an apology, Eleanor would have been terribly disappointed. The other woman's lips puckered as she held a slice of lemon between her teeth. She felt the slide of snakelike eyes move over her slowly, deciding she was being wickedly unfair to snakes with the comparison, the other woman's gaze at last settling on Eleanor's face. She gave a dubious little snort, her eyes moving in a quick up and down once again.

"Are you quite certain?"

Fire bloomed in her veins, and she wondered if she could possibly break the record for ruining her own chances of success with this ball.

The other woman sniffed, turning away as if Eleanor were no longer worthy of her undivided attention. "Well, you can hardly blame me. If you go traipsing about dressed like the help, you can't be surprised when someone assumes you are, in fact, the help. I think my gardener has that same dress."

Her mouth dropped open, but she couldn't even bring herself to gasp in offense. She was too shocked at the woman's brazenness. Before she could react, a lanky young man with foppish brown curls appeared. "Darling, the maid brought your tea." He gave Eleanor the same swift up and down with a similarly sour expression.

"Finally! It's been ages since I asked . . ." The duo gave Eleanor one last wrinkled-nose look before disappearing down the corridor. *Unbelievable.* If that's what the rest of the ball was going to be like, she would need to identify her best match, seal the deal as quickly as possible, and encourage him to leave early.

"Miss?" She jumped in surprise at the unexpected voice, the diminutive fox-eared appearing at her elbow. "Miss Eastwick," she gave a bobbing curtsy that sent her fluffy tail bouncing, "I'm Trilby. I'll be your ladies' maid for the ball. Let me show you to your room, miss."

The girl was debutante-aged herself, Eleanor realized that she followed the young woman. Eyeing the various seams in the fox girl's dress, allowing her tail to come through, she thought, quite unwillingly, up Silas. Unbuttoning his tailcoat had been oddly intimate, especially considering the reason why she was unbuttoning it and what they were doing together, but for some reason, that specific act seemed even more emotionally charged to her. The actions of a wife, she thought, cheeks heating.

"Do you know who that was?" Eleanor asked once the door had clicked shut behind them. "Those two people I was talking to, the man and the woman?"

Trilby's smile was tight as she nodded her head, all the answer Eleanor needed. "The Skevingtons. Lady Stephana is here to attend the ball, and her brother Archie is here as her chaperone." *Perfect. Names to avoid.* "I'll begin unpacking all of your trunks, miss. Do you have a preference on which dress you would like to have for dinner?"

She had packed her best dresses. The nicest was from her own days as a dewy-faced debutante, although it had been altered several times to accommodate the curves she hadn't had when the dress was first commissioned. None of her dresses or gowns were particularly well-tailored, not anymore. They had been taken apart and turned so many times, never to her exact measurements, and she already knew that she would be the most shabbily dressed attendee the ball would likely see. *Which is why the marquis's lessons are going to be so important.*

"There's only one trunk, so you won't have much to—"

She turned, her mouth dropping open in shock at what lay at the foot of the bed. Her own small valise, looking positively ancient amidst the sumptuously appointed chamber, as the fox girl rooted through the first of two other opened trunks that she had never seen before. "Oh dear, Trilby, I believe there's been a mistake . . ."

"If you weren't certain, miss, I think this light purple is lovely. It'll bring out your eyes. It will be a nice counterpoint to your outfit for the masked ball."

Eleanor floundered. She had no idea what purple dress she was meant to own, nor what costume she was meant to wear to this masked ball. "Master Bow mentioned that there would be masks on hand if needed?"

"Oh yes, Master Bow thinks of everything. Fortunately, you won't be needing it with your own lovely dress here. If you've no objections, I'll take the lavender out now and ensure it is ready for dinner."

She watched the young fox woman remove a beautiful, wisteria-colored gown from the trunk that was absolutely not hers.

"Here's your letter, Miss." Trilby removed an envelope from the trunk, and Eleanor was shocked that it did, in fact, bear her name.

My dearest Eleanor,

I hope this trunk finds you well. I had it sent ahead of the ball to ensure it would be there upon your arrival. I confess, I had to solicit help from my housekeeper, but she herself is a vicious woman with admirable style, and I am confident we selected well for you, my dear. Lucy and your maid were most helpful in providing your measurements.

I'm so pleased to hear that Lord Stride was amenable to our request, and I've no doubt he has left you in an admirable position to secure the match you're looking for. My only regret is that I have not been able to do more. I so wish your father would have asked for help years ago, and I wish I had learned of your situation earlier, but there is no sense in dwelling on what is done. We all must look to the future and find happier times for ourselves and those we love.

I am confident that this is a good match, my dear Eleanor. It may not have seemed so at the beginning, but you are a vibrant young woman with an adventurous soul, and I can think of no better way to keep that spark in you lit. I greatly am looking forward to receiving the announcement of your engagement, my dear.

All of my love,

Uncle Efraim.

Tears spilled over her cheeks. She was likely meant to have read this after the ball, she realized, for Uncle Efraim spoke as if her match had already been made. She watched as Trilby removed several gowns from the trunk — the aforementioned wisteria, a stunning ivory confection that was the most sophisticated thing she had ever owned, and an evening dress of soft mauve with a lace inset all the way to the bottom hem.

She took the dress from Trilby, holding it up herself and gazing into the mirror. It was lovely. The young fox woman was right — the color was stunning. It was also a rather conservative style, somewhat high-necked, with clean lines rather than being overly adorned with fripperies. Silas Stride would tell her she was dressing like an 80-year-old woman again, and she swallowed down a laugh. It didn't matter. The dresses, all three of them, were beautiful. They were a sight better than what she had brought from home, and even with the conservative style, she could still make them work.

"It's lovely, miss. A bit severe, but a stunning color." Trilby cocked her head, tapping her mouth with a long, segmented finger. "Seeing as you're trying to get a husband, miss, if you wanted to make it a bit naughty, we can dampen your chemise."

The laugh that escaped her was like a bark, and Eleanor clapped a hand over her mouth to contain it, but it was too late. Her shoulders shook, and her eyes watered. She and this maid were going to get along very, very well.

The second trunk was larger. The first dress Trilby pulled out made Eleanor gasp. It was a day dress of emerald green, a bold, audacious color, in a modern cut with a low neckline and puffed sleeves. There was a pleated fan trim twisted around the bodice, zigzagging over the skirt, ending in a puddle of ruffles at the bottom hem. It was ridiculously ornate and beautiful, but she had no idea where it had come from. Three more dresses followed, all in bright colors and daring cuts, with painted lace and hand-beaded trim, feathers and ruffles and extravagance.

There were matching fans and shoes, reticules and parasols, and then at the bottom, the pièce de résistance. A dove grey gown of satin. The bodice was adorned with beads and pearls and swirling embroidery, the most opulent things she'd ever seen in her life. Grey satin slippers, a grey tulle fan . . . and a cape that was heavy with beadwork, the embroidery floss so dense that it caused a separation in the gauzy chiffon panels, forming — she gasped, realizing what it was. The two panels formed rounded wings that draped over her shoulders and down her back. The finishing effect was a silver-grey domino mask with bouncing feathered antennae. *Let me hear you sing, little moth.*

"There's a letter with this too, miss. Do you want it as well?"

She held out a shaky hand, unable to reconcile the heap of extravagant dresses she had just been sent for a three-day affair.

Dear Miss Eastwick,

I am ridiculously upset with my brute of a brother for not notifying me of when your departure was. He has informed me that you will be leaving this morning, and your bags are already packed. I don't know if this trunk will make it in time to be included with the rest of your things. In the event that it is not, I am sending it posthaste to Dorset in hopes that it will arrive shortly after your arrival.

Enclosed you will find several dresses, some for day and some for evening, all with the appropriate accessories. I do hope that you will not look at this gift as an act of charity, nor as though I am casting off my old hand-me-downs, for it is neither. Yes, these dresses have all been worn by me and me alone. But you see, they are not mere hand-me-downs.

I love each item in this trunk. They were all gifts from our dearest brother, from his travels abroad. None of them currently fit me, and seeing them ignored in my wardrobe brings my heart sorrow. I've been told by my midwife that I'm unlikely to return to my previous size once my child is born, especially if I am planning on having another as soon as possible, which I am.

None of these gowns were commissioned for state affairs or Royal balls. None of them were anything other than gifts to me, purchased with love. I do not wish to see them sitting unused and unappreciated until they are moth-eaten, and inevitably, styles will change too dramatically for my own daughter to be able to enjoy them. So I would like you to have them, Miss Eastwick. I want to see these things that I love find new life with someone who will appreciate them for what they are — a token of appreciation, with no strings attached.

It was lovely meeting you, and I do hope your time at the ball ends beneficially for all of us. I look forward to seeing you again very soon.

Affectionately yours,

Lady Maris Stride

She was speechless for several long moments. She had met Silas's striking younger sister only once, but it had been enough to leave a strong impression. Maris Stride did not suffer fools, her brother included, that was evident.

She had been on her way to the moon temple the first and only time she had encountered Lady Maris, her arms full of his clothes. She was still furious with him. She was still angry and humiliated and hurt, and she reminded him of what would happen once she left the Monster's Ball at every opportunity — all of his lessons would be applied to another man, and all of his tips on seduction and lovemaking would be used on someone else. She could see that it rankled him, and that soothed the ache in her heart . . . But beneath the ache, she was still in love with him. There was no denying that. He was a rake and a reprobate, and he had made it clear he was not interested in marriage, but she did not possess a hard enough heart to forget how soft he made her feel.

His chamber servants had been utterly perplexed by her request for his lordship's clothes at first, but now they had them ready. It was an abominably improper way to behave, particularly in front of the servants who likely all had wagging tongues, but she didn't care. *In another few days, it wouldn't matter.* Dressing him was the most intimate thing she had ever done.

"I apologize for forgetting the powder. I hope your arse can survive the evening, my lord," she had tittered, holding out his breeches as if he were a child who needed help stepping into them.

"Give me that," he had huffed, snatching them from her. She had giggled the entire time he dressed, mumbling to himself over the lack of the looking glass. Fastening the snaps around his wings was the only thing he truly needed assistance with, and she did so, fastening his shirt and waistcoat and, finally, his jacket. She straightened his collar and pushed his hair into place with her fingers.

"Did you even bring any pomade? I'm certain my hair looks a fright."

"Oh, your hair looks fine. Who are you trying to impress anyway?" As soon as the words were out, Eleanor nearly swallowed her tongue. She wondered if he had been trying to impress *her* all these weeks, or if the Marquis of Basingstone simply didn't leave his perch without looking as if a team of servants had buffed and manicured every inch of him.

That evening she was hurrying up the stone pathway, later than she normally left, when she stopped short at the sight of the beautiful, ornately dressed woman. She could tell immediately it was his sister. Aside from the fact that she was a striking gargoyle of black marble, she was heavy with child. Her silvery white hair was thick and elaborately plaited around her head, and the dress she wore was mind-bogglingly opulent. Silas Stride had the bearing of an arrogant dandy, but his sister had the bearing of a queen.

"Good evening, dear. It's a lovely night, isn't it?

"It is, my lady. I apologize if I startled you."

"Not at all dear. I've always been a bit of an early riser compared to my brother. I take it you are the guest I've heard about? Lord Ellingboe's sponsor?"

"Yes, my lady. Eleanor Eastwick, I'm very pleased to make your acquaintance. You're the marquis's sister. May I say your dress is absolutely stunning? It looks like something from another age."

Her laugh was as shimmering and icy as her brother's. "Oh, my dear girl, flattery will get you absolutely everywhere, especially with a pregnant woman. Come, walk with me. Yes, I'm the infamous Lady Maris. I take it you are heading to the moon temple? Are those my brother's clothes? Doesn't he have a manservant to dress him?"

"Oh, I'm certain he has at least several of those. A servant to feed him, one to dress him, another to bathe him. Likely one to powder his arse, is what I told him."

Maris Stride had the giddy laughter of a teenage girl, and it bounced off the arbor as they walked up the path. "No one has ever claimed that my darling brother was not a fop," she laughed, linking her arm with Eleanor's and wiping at her eyes with the other. "Mercy, I'm supposed to be avoiding stimulation. I'm going to be borrowing that line in the future, Miss Eastwick. So we know he is a fop, and we know he has a bevy of servants to attend to his every need, isolating him from ever truly needing to grow up."

"Do men ever truly need to grow up, Lady Maris?"

"No. They do not. And isn't that the point? We have to marry them to secure our futures. I understand you are seeking a husband, Miss Eastwick. Lord Ellingboe wrote to me some time ago. I hope that you have found what you're looking for."

She had turned then, uncertain of what his sister meant.

"Come now, Miss Eastwick. We've established that my brother is a spoiled child, and yet here you are, on your way to dress him yourself. Are you in love with him?"

The whole world had seemed to sway in that moment. The twisting vines of the orchard and the trees bordering the nearby forest, the sea tipped, and the moon swung. "I don't see how it matters," she answered finally.

"Does it not? It seems to me like that would matter quite a bit."

Eleanor shook her head, afraid to speak lest her tears crowded her throat. "No, it does not. I have two younger sisters and an agéd grandmother, and barely a farthing to my name, Lady Stride. It doesn't matter if I love your brother if he's not going to marry me. I need to secure my family's future. I'm sure you understand."

"Oh, I do, dear girl. A woman's burden is never-ending. It is the one thing that transcends species. It makes no matter if one is human or minotaur or orcish or gargoyle. The burden falls on us to pick up the pieces when our menfolk cannot, which is always. The burden is on us to forge alliances and bear children and provide heirs, and for all our sacrifice, we get very little in return. I completely understand your reasoning, Miss Eastwick. I hope you're able to find a lord who is at least a little worthy of you."

To receive such a generous gift now tightened her throat.

"This ivory would be lovely to wear to breakfast tomorrow, miss. Especially with her ladyship in attendance."

She sucked in a long breath and looked around. Her room was on the third floor, and she knew that in the grand hierarchy of these sorts of events, that was a slight. But not one that she decided to care about. *You are untitled and a pauper. Just be glad you're here.* And now, she had a dragon's hoard of lovely dresses, the likes of which she had never owned, even when things were good. *From pauper to princess.* The only question was, were any of them bold enough to heat the blood of one of these monstrous lords. *The scandal is the point.* Eleanor shook her head, clearing the space between her ears of the cobwebs of his voice.

"Ivory is perfect for breakfast. And obviously, the moth for the ball tonight and the purple for dinner. We'll take stock of what to wear tomorrow afternoon once we decide what we will be doing."

The moment before taking the stage was pregnant with anxiety. It didn't matter where she was singing. It didn't matter what she was thinking. It didn't matter if she was simply introducing someone else or following the pianist to his bench in order to shuffle music as he played. It wasn't the same as the moment before the music started. It was the existence of the *maybe*.

Maybe a scrim would fall in the midst of her aria, or maybe she would tread too close to the edge of the stage and go tumbling into the orchestra pit. Maybe the crowd would be empty; maybe it would be full of hecklers and blackguards who would not hesitate to boo a missed note. Maybe it would be a great triumph . . . Or maybe she would be a laughingstock. The moment before taking the stage was so horrid because there were any number of ways the evening could progress and no scrying stone to tell her what lay in store.

It was how she felt as they were introduced one by one. She'd entered into the queue behind the two

other women with rooms on her corridor – a lovely, dark-haired young woman with her chaperone beside her and a bookish-looking redhead with furtive
eyes. She spied the horrid shrew from earlier that day
– Stephana Skevington — and a host of other lovely women there in their best dresses, all angling for
the same thing — a monstrous husband. Some of the
women looked anxious, while others looked as if they
were champing at the bit. A handful looked as if they
would rather be anywhere else in the world, and one or
two, she thought, looked near tears.

It was the first opportunity any of the men in attendance would have to see them, and she hoped that
the lovely purple dress showed off her assets well. Trilby had indeed dampened her chemise, soaking until it
was dripping, and hanging it to dry some so as not to
completely spoil her dress. She had wound up dressing
twice. The first time she donned the wisteria satin, the
fox girl had frowned, shaking her head.

"Not wet enough, miss. It's not giving us the effect
you want."

Over her head came the dress, and Trilby scooped
handfuls of water from the washbasin, patting it onto

the bodice of her chemise until she was satisfied with the moisture level. When she turned away to dry her hands, Eleanor took advantage of the moment to pinch her nipples, coaxing them to hardness. *After all, isn't that the point? The scandal?*

When the dress was pulled back over her head and each tiny pearl button fastened, Trilby beamed in triumph. "If catching a husband is your aim, miss, you'll be beating them off with a stick tonight."

And now she stood waiting, waiting for her name to be called, for her presentation to the rest of the ballroom, for the moment of truth. She was not the only one with a dampened dress, she was almost relieved to see. She wondered what the lord would catch her eye. Perhaps the orc she was anticipating, or maybe something completely foreign to her, like a minotaur or serpent. Her heart was thumping in her chest like a timpani, and her lungs felt crowded. Not butterflies this time. *Moths.* It was the herky-jerky movement of moths fluttering within her, nervous and weaving, bumping into her lungs in their clumsy panic. *You only have to get through this moment once. You can't afford to trip and fall. You are doing this for the girls.*

"Miss Eleanor Eastwick, daughter of the late Philip Exeter Eastwick, Esquire, of London."

Stepping to the center of the grand staircase, she smiled in a way that she hoped conveyed she was both a lady and a seductress, and an excellent candidate for marriage. She kept her eyes on the unfamiliar steps, looking out at the small sea of potential suitors on every third one. There was indeed a minotaur, she saw, as well as the long, twisting tail of a serpent. There was a reserved-looking man who cast a blue glow, and the lord standing beside him had the long ears of a rabbit.

And there, directly in her line of sight, with the same lofty look and half-smirk he'd worn for the majority of the past month, was the Marquis of Basingstone. Silas Stride smiled as their eyes met, shining sapphires and blinding white fang, upending her heart and all of her plans.

The High Tea

SOCIETY PAPERS

Greetings, sweet sippers!

Kettles are whistling with all the buzz from the Monsters Ball, dear readers! Our keen eyes have spotted none other than the Marquis of Basingstone in attendance at this first bête monde soirée of the season — — our all-seeing serving spoons have told us he's come to claim the heart of none other than one of the failed diamonds of the season, not a stranger to these pages.

Could she be the mystery woman this unrepentant rake was entertaining over these last weeks? Is our favorite stony-hearted libertine ready to trade in his ever-rotating dance card for a marriage license?

Do mind the temperature and sip slowly as this story unfolds, dear readers!

Lady Grey

Silas

She had dampened her dress. He might have laughed at the audacious brazenness had he been the lone recipient of the after-effects. As it was, he'd hardly been able to pull his eyes away from the creamy round globes of her beautiful breasts, her heavy, luscious tits that he loved so much, that place between them where he wanted to live forever, on display and advertised for the lascivious enjoyment every other lord in the room.

It was his own fault. He had told her, in the beginning, that she would need to be bold, that she would need to secure the favor of one of these noblemen by way of their cock. She was bright and witty and sparkling, and he had no doubt that all of the other charms she possessed would win over whoever set their sights on her, but in a crowded playing field with other women of the same aim, she would need to be bold to set herself apart. She'd taken his words seriously.

That was, of course, before he loved her. To be given the opportunity to rewind the past month, he would've encouraged her to dress like a vestal virgin at the ball, to behave modestly, to have a chaperone with her at all times, and to never, ever allow one of these desperate dandies to put their hands on her. Now it was too late. She had put her beautiful curves on display for the highest bidder in this chattel auction, and she would likely be fielding offers all night.

"Didn't think I'd be seeing you here, Stride." The laconic drawl came from the trollish lord beside him, the second son of a baron, whose elder brother had recently taken ill, according to the High Tea. "I do hope you've not come to simply sample all of the ladies in attendance before flitting off. I believe the Countess has strict rules over her ball being used as a catalog for common rakes."

Silas grinned. He was here to claim his bride, but he still had a reputation to keep up. "Good to see you,

Morrington. My condolences to your family. I hear your brother is not doing well at all. I see they're officially calling in your spare card." The troll glowered, and Silas's smile stretched. "As another member of the second son's club, I welcome you to the fold. But I *do* hope you are going to explain to whichever young lady you set your sights on that you are merely the emergency option."

She was descending the steps, and he no longer had an interest in the troll. Their eyes locked, and Silas desperately wished he could have said that hers were full of joy at the sight of him, but that, too, would have been a pretty lie he was telling himself. She looked shocked. Shocked and angry, but he reminded himself that was to be expected. The rest of the ladies were called as they came down the steps, but he paid attention to none of them. The only woman in the room he was interested in was having her hand kissed by a minotaur, and his blood boiled.

The presentation and then dinner, a brief respite for the ladies to change, and then the masked ball, that was the agenda for the night. He would claim her at dinner; no sense in delaying what needed to happen. These balls were a tricky social maneuver. Chatting with a lady over dinner was only polite; giving her your undivided attention, however, was a marker of clear interest shown. To dance with a lady at the ball was, again, a nicety that was observed by all in attendance. To dance with her a second time immediately after was to stake a claim, an announcement to all in attendance that you were an interested party, and they should keep their distance. Silas was prepared to enter the dining room and stake her out, claim the chair next to her, and not allow another lord in attendance to so much as blink in her direction . . . but fate was not smiling at him that evening.

"Lords and ladies, please pay attention to your place settings. We have designed tonight's seating chart specifically and would appreciate adherence." The master of ceremonies was a beaming man with the shining eyes of a shifter of some sort, and finding his place clear across the table from Eleanor's, Silas desperately wanted to fling his water goblet in the man's direction.

"It's so ridiculous that they have allowed such rabble in this year," sniffed the woman seated beside him. She was tall and thin with a long neck and dark hair, and a permanently sour expression, he thought. She was seated across from a man who looked to be her age or maybe just a year or so older, clearly a relation, likely her chaperone.

Silas was too busy staring across the table at Eleanor, who was now being chatted up by a lagomorph to her left. Morrington was across from her. *That's a small favor, at least. He doesn't have a pot to piss in.* "Why, just this afternoon, I was asking one of the servants to bring me some tea, only to find out that it was actually a guest! She was dressed like a scullery maid. I don't see how it's appropriate to trot out a chit like that in front of genteel society. And I've heard there are second sons in attendance who don't even have titles of their own. Really, must we stoop so low?"

She looked at Silas pointedly, and he realized he was expected to participate in the conversation. "Who are you?" The question was out before he could frame it more politely, deciding that the woman was being so rude he didn't actually care. If her story was true, she was speaking of one of the other young ladies in attendance which was exceptionally poor form, particularly considering that his Eleanor was likely to not be the most well-heeled amongst this crowd.

"Lord Archibald Skevington," answered the man at her side, sniffing as though he were the crown prince himself. "And this is my sister, Lady Stephana."

"The Lord of what?" Silas asked bluntly. "Your name is not one I recognize, sir, although admittedly, I don't know every human lord. But I've not heard anyone address you as your grace, nor as the lord *of* anything."

He raised a sardonic eyebrow as the man sputtered. The woman at his side looked thoroughly horrified.

"Forgive me, but it seems you yourself are using a courtesy title. You'll have to excuse me for saying so, but it seems a bit odd, *my lord*, to speak ill of those doing the same. For example, I am *the* Marquis of Basingstone. The only people in this room who rank higher than me are to be addressed as your grace, like his grace, the Duke of Sackwell," he gestured to the duke sitting across the table, someone he'd known since childhood. "So if we are, in fact, holding those with lesser titles to a lesser degree of civility, I don't think either of you should be speaking to me or his grace. Do you see the way that works?"

Across the table, Sackwell chuckled. "It doesn't make a difference what that paper says about you, Stride. You are always the most amusing dinner guest."

The rest of the excruciating dinner passed quickly enough, and then ladies were being whisked away. When they returned to the ballroom for the dancing, he would make his move. Monopolize her. *Don't let another one of these charlatans put a finger on her.*

When they reentered the ballroom, the sight of her almost stopped his heart as effectively as the afternoon sun. She was resplendent. She looked as ethereal as a moon goddess, dressed in silvery gray, the beaded cape she wore forming wide wings at her back. A moth, he realized, his heart seeming to tap at the back of his tongue. He recognized the costume. It was something of Maris's. The dress had never fit her especially well, but she would wear the wings and the mask to afternoon tea, looking absolutely absurd sipping her lemonade with the antennae bobbing about her face, not that she could ever be told anything. Eleanor, on the other hand, looked completely precious. Alluring and goddess-like, and there was no time like the present to announce his intentions.

"May I join you in this dance, my lady?"

Her head jerked up from the conversation in which she'd been engaged, and her eyes flashed at him mutinously. *She's only surprised, that's all.*

"What are you doing here, Lord Stride?" The question was asked through her teeth, and even then, when she was clearly furious, her face red with anger and her eyes bright with fury, she was absolutely the most beautiful woman in the entire world.

"I'm a member of the monstrous peerage, Miss Eastwick. Why wouldn't I be here?"

She had no choice but to accept his request to dance, although it was clear she wanted to tell him to sod off. They were the third couple in the quadrille they joined, and Silas was positive she was going to snatch a candle from the nearest candelabra and set him on fire.

"It just seems odd to me," she continued in the same tight voice, "that you never thought of *mentioning* your attendance at any point in the past month, my lord. Up to and including this *very* morning when you said goodbye as if it was the last time we would ever see each other."

The music started, and they were forced to play their roles. A bow and a curtsy, waiting their turn to join the square. "Little moth, it's important to tell the people you care about that you do so each day. You were undertaking a long journey. I would never leave it to chance that I would have the opportunity to voice my appreciation for the time we've spent together. You look stunningly beautiful, by the way."

She did not have a chance to respond, for they were moving then, light hopping steps, his hand at her waist and her nails digging into the fine cloth of his coat as if she wished they could tear at his skin. It was a fast-paced dance, and she avoided eye contact with him throughout. He had known she would be surprised to see him, and her anger was not unjustified. But they needed to work through it quickly before one of these other jackanapes set his sights on her.

"My dear, did you *dampen* your dress? I am positively scandalized and so entirely proud of your progress under my tutelage in such a short amount of time." He was positive she growled at him — *growled*! — and her adorable display of rage was quite possibly the most endearing thing he'd ever experienced. They'd reached the end of their circuit, bowing again.

"Well, my lord, someone should've told you." She stretched up on her tiptoes, pulling the lapels of his jacket until he bent enough for her to reach his ear. "The scandal is the point."

The dance ended, and applause rang through the ballroom.

"May I have anoth —"

"You may *not*. Dancing twice in a row with a single partner is an indication of a preference, my lord, a fact you well know. Now please, Lord Stride, I beg you — do not destroy my chances at success."

He somehow found himself at a table full of what he presumed were similarly jilted prospects. "Roth," he barked at a familiar glowing face. "Good to see you out and about, your grace."

"Stride, you're the very last bachelor in London I would expect to see at an event like this." The speaker was a laconic naga, one whose trials with his ex-wife had been thoroughly covered by the High Tea.

"I suppose none of us need to wonder why *you're* here, Casselon."

The viscount grinned, his fangs shining in the candlelight. "No, I suppose not. All of London has had a front-row seat. Rather like the exploits of your bedroom."

Silas laughed, unable to argue. She was dancing with the minotaur, then an orc with a ridiculously outdated coat, chattering with a red-haired young woman against the far wall for a bit, and then somehow, in the minotaur's arms again.

"Stride, you look positively green with envy. Don't tell me you're seriously here with your eye on someone."

"Oh, I am, Warwick. I am going home engaged, and I am going to turn that Minotaur into the *finest* pair of leather boots if his hand slips any further. But first, I am going to get very slightly drunk."

Eleanor

He was ruining all of her plans.

It should have been easy, snagging one of these enthusiastic, eager lords. The minotaur seemed especially keen, but she wasn't sure if she could get over his bovine snout. The orc lord in attendance was thick with muscle and stately-looking, but also deadly dull, and rather than assessing her choices thoroughly with a cool head, the looming presence of Silas Stride kept pulling her attention. She didn't know why he was here, but if he didn't disappear rather quickly, she was going to find wherever it was he slept and push him into the lake.

"What do you ladies fancy doing tomorrow," the rabbit-eared man asked gaily to the cluster of giggling women around him. Silas was there, edging around the back end of the group, and she felt as if she were being circled.

"It will surely be a fine day to go riding, ladies." That was from the orc. She tried to focus on the breadth of his shoulders and the thickness of his thighs and not the boringness of his conversation and his lack of witty repartee. She danced with him twice that evening, well spaced so as not to show that she was overly interested. Each time had felt as though she were trapped, sinking in the thick mud of the lowlands, and it was a relief when the music ended, freeing her. *Do you want to be entertained? Or do you want to feed your family, you silly little fool!*

"It's been many years since I've been riding, my lord, but if you don't mind a novice in tow, that sounds like a delightful way to spend the morning."

"Miss Eastwick, I did not take you for such an enthusiastic horsewoman." It was *him*, of course. Eleanor turned her dagger-like grin to Silas, hoping he noticed it was more of a grimace.

"I take it you don't ride, my Lord?"

Instantly, his icy eyes brightened, and his treacherous mouth curled. Eleanor castigated herself the moment the words were out. The other monstrous men were a league below him. Unlike nearly every other lord she'd spoken with that evening, the Marquis of Basingstone was not one she could spar with and hope to walk away without feeling as though he had unfastened her to her very core.

"My dear Miss Eastwick, if having a beast between your thighs is your desire, I can think of a setting to which the two of us might adjourn that's far worthier than a manure and mud-soaked field. I should be happy to provide you ample opportunity to play the horse-woman."

Her face flamed as he leaned in closer, his whisper for ears alone.

"And besides, my dear, the stink of the stable is still on him, despite that wretched fragrance he's attempted to use to cover it. He's not interested in playing horsey the same way we have. I thought I'd already shown you that, but I'm happy to repeat the lesson at home."

She hated that she wanted to laugh. *No, we just hate him.* She circled away putting distance between herself and his sharp blue eyes.

"I was thinking perhaps we could row on the lake, Miss Eastwick." That was the minotaur. Unlike the orc, he had been a genial conversationalist. He had also been a genial conversationalist with every other woman in attendance, and she had a feeling he would continue to be a genial conversationalist with other women well after he finally found a bride. *Do we care? As long as the girls are taken care of, who cares how far his hand wanders.*

"He's a regular attendee of these balls, little moth." A hiss at her ear, Silas having found her again, the smell of him clouding her head. "I'm not sure why he's not been able to seal the deal, but something keeps alerting the other young ladies. I would greatly prefer that you didn't have to find out whatever that was when you are alone, and I'm certain the earl would agree. Besides, if you want to go rowing, I have a beautiful lake at Basingstone, and I'm told there are swans."

She stamped her foot, noticing too late that the action was witnessed by the blue-glowing man and the countess. She didn't care. He was lucky she wasn't stomping on his face.

"Are you alright?" It was Penney, the girl from her floor, who preferred books to the idea of marriage, smiling in concern.

"I-I, yes, I'm fine. I'm just incredibly *vexed* at the moment."

He was trailing after her like a stray cat, and he had something to say about every man in attendance. He knew them all, of course, and had known them all for years, no doubt. He knew their peculiarities and their perversions, and under different circumstances, she would quite welcome his counsel . . . But it seemed he was determined to turn her away from every potential suitor. It was only the first night, she reminded herself, but considering the ball was only three days long and engagement announcements would be made upon the third, it seemed like no time at all.

She noticed her bookish new friend engaged in conversation with the blue flame man a short while later, and her other neighbor, the lovely woman with her chaperone, was being entertained by the serpent. She was not the only woman in attendance who was not yet definitively paired off, for there was a handful of the regular wallflowers these events always attracted and few others like her, yet undecided.

"Miss Eastwick, I crave the opportunity to speak with you privately."

She closed her eyes and sucked in a breath between her teeth, avoiding having to smell his familiar, comfortable scent.

"I can't imagine what it is you have to say, my Lord, considering you had two weeks in which to do so. The full month, technically. You were asked by the Earl to assist me, and you assisted. I thank you for your help, and if repayment is what you seek, I assure you, my Lord, I will find a way to do so. But if you do not leave me be and let me find a husband this weekend, Lord Stride, I promise you that I will return to Basingstone in the middle of the day with every pigeon in London and introduce them to the roof of the moon temple."

His laughter was still an icy white slide of satin, gliding up the back of her neck. "Little moth, please. I'm begging you. Please meet me at the hedge maze after the next quadrille."

He vanished from her side after that, and she allowed herself to be pulled into the dance by the lagomorph. He was charming and funny, and as she moved through the dance with him, the orc catching her eye as he watched their quadrille from the side, she wondered why it was that she was not putting her whole heart into a single potential match. *Because next to* **him***, they're all dull and unamusing. Because none of them infuriate you and excite you at the same time. Because none of them are him.*

"Miss Eastwick? If you're looking for the hedge maze, the doors at the other end of the ballroom would be most expeditious." The countess gave her another one of those knowing, cat-like grins, motioning to the doors in question, and Eleanor paused, wondering whose side she was even on.

She slipped out the doors, after navigating her way through the crowded ballroom, sucking in a lungful of the cool night air. Leaving during the dancing was the done thing, he had said. Pausing at the top of the stone staircase, Elanor looked out at the wide expanse of the grounds before her. They were not the only couple to have taken to the outdoors. She could see them pairing off, headed to the lake, the sculpture garden, and the fountain. *Pairing off, which meant already paired.* And here she was, partnerless, preparing to argue with Silas Stride. *You've ruined everything. You may as well go home now and start looking for cleaning work.*

"Miss Eastwick."

She startled the sound of his voice, turning to find him there, a soft smile curving his lips.

"I saw you coming. The hedge maze is that way," he gestured over his shoulder. "I thought you might be headed to the lake."

"Well, I don't exactly know my way around, particularly in the dark. What is it that you wanted to speak with me about, Lord Stride? Why did you follow me? Do you hate me so much, my lord?"

"Hate you? My dear girl, why would you even say something like that? Quite the contrary, I lo —"

"Why would I say that?" She backed up, incredulous. "Why would I say that? What else am I supposed to think?! You *know* how important this is. This isn't a game for me, Lord Stride. This is a matter of my entire family's survival, and you know that. And yet here you are, actively sabotaging my every move. What else am I supposed to think?"

"Miss Eastwick, please. You're right, I am getting in the way of you making a match with another lord. Why would you marry them? Why not *me*, Eleanor? You've been a guest at my home, you know that I am well-provisioned to take care of a family, to raise a family. Some of the lords here tonight are practically paupers, with a title and little else. You know I can take care of you. Your sisters will be well-educated as the finest young ladies, and your grandmother can enjoy her golden years with every comfort at her disposal. I love you, Eleanor. I've come to claim you as my bride, Miss Eastwick, and bring you home to Basingstone, where you belong."

She was speechless. It was the last thing she expected him to say, and while it might have been what she was pining for a brief moment two weeks ago, now all she felt was fury.

"You . . . love me. *Now*, you love me. Now that I'm here, trying to make a change for the better in my life. Not at any point in the last month, but now." A red mist swam over her eyes, and she could barely control her actions as she pounced on him, gripping the lapels of his jacket. "I wouldn't marry you if you were the last man in London with a pulse, my lord. You had every opportunity to let me know *this* is what you were thinking, and you did nothing. You did nothing but remind me that all that was between us were *lessons*. You had me in your bed, and you could have claimed me as yours then."

She was livid with him and even more furious with herself for the hot tears that spilled down her cheeks, crowding her throat and nearly making speech impossible. "You could have asked me to stay forever that night, and I would have said yes, Silas. I would've said yes a hundred times over. But you didn't. You didn't tell me you loved me then. You didn't ask me to stay. You let me leave. And then you went to a brothel." He looked ill at her words, and her breath was hitching with the force of holding in her sob, but she was undaunted.

"You had the opportunity to show me exactly what kind of man you are, Silas Stride, and you did so. *Love* me. I don't think you even know the meaning of the word. You're a spoiled child. You only want me now because someone else may have me. And if I were to say yes right now and leave with you tonight, you would be bored by the time we even returned to Basingstone, and you would throw me away like a tatty little plaything. I would accept all that and worse from any single one of the lords in that room because I don't know them, and I don't *care* about them. But you . . . I *did* care for you. But you didn't care for anything but your own debauchery. You don't even know what love is. I don't ever want to see you again, Silas Stride."

"Eleanor? Dear, are you joining us for breakfast?"

The voice made her sit up with a startle. Her head was swimming, a dull ache forming behind her eye, the result of the previous evening's tears. She had nearly cried herself sick before pulling herself together and returning to the ballroom. *You're not doing this for you.*

She'd made plans with the orc lord to go riding after breakfast, Master Bow swooping in with the excellent news that he would hunt down a riding habit for her to borrow. After tea, she was meant to row on the lake with the rabbit-eared lordling whom she'd mentally dubbed Lord Hops-a-lot, a moniker she was certain he'd not appreciate. First though, was breakfast on the verandah with the countess and the other guests, to which she'd enthusiastically agreed . . . not remembering that normal people had breakfast at an ungodly early hour.

"Eleanor?" It was Penelope, her sweet, bookish neighbor.

"Yes," she croaked. "I-I'm just finishing dressing. I'll be along in a moment."

Trilby came bustling in then, pulling back the covers. "I didn't think you were getting up today, miss. Sleeping like a stone, you were."

By the time she made it out on the verandah, the sun was high and blinding. Her head ached. She had no idea how people did this each day. It certainly couldn't have been healthy. She'd feel her retinas searing in the morning light, wondering why they couldn't simply move breakfast to a more respectable time, say, half two.

"I'm looking forward to riding with you this morning, my lady." The orc lord was upright and formal. A stiff upper lip, her grandmother would have said. "I have a rather impressive stable back home, so if riding is one of your passions, you'll be well-provisioned."

She was positive she had mentioned to this lord the previous evening that she had not been on a horse in some time, so it was hardly appropriate to assume that riding was one of her passions. "Are you a fan of music, my lord?"

"I can't say that I am, no. After a long day overseeing my land and men, I prefer a quiet house in the evenings before retiring."

He would be a perfect match. After all, according to Silas, you dress like an 80-year-old woman, and he behaves like an 80-year-old man.

The sun was worse once they set out on the horses. Her head was throbbing, the pain behind her eye all-encompassing, and with each bounce against the saddle, it seemed to lance into her brain. The pain became so severe, at one point she was certain she was going to fall and required the orc lord's assistance in keeping her seat on the return trip. Eleanor could tell she had not impressed him, but at the moment, she didn't care. *A silent home and a bridegroom that smells like his horse groom. You'll do better with Lord Hops-a-lot.*

She was meeting him at the lake, and once she had changed into one of the lovely day dresses Maris Stride had provided, Eleanor set off, shaded beneath her green parasol. She was early and decided to take advantage of the shade beneath the tree not far from the lake. Sitting in the grass, she decided her headache might go away if she rested for a bit. Now it was dusk. The sun was puddling into a smear of crimson at the horizon over the water, above a wash of indigo, and a stripe of apricot above the bleeding sun. She had missed rowing. She had missed rowing and whatever other activities were planned for the early evening.

The only consolation, small as it was, was that her headache was gone. The grounds seemed deserted, and she realized everyone was likely already in their rooms, dressing for dinner. *And here you are, just waking for the night.*

She knew exactly which building he would've chosen to make his perch. She'd taken note of it while they were riding. It was set back, well behind the lake, nearing the cliffs. She thought it must've been a lookout at one point, but it would've served his purpose admirably. The nearby forest was far enough to prevent any shade from touching the rooftop of the structure, and it was far enough away from the main house for him to sleep peacefully.

She couldn't explain why her feet carried her down the hill, past the lake where she was meant to row with the other lord, down the pathway that took her through the sculpture garden and around the hedge maze, skirting on the side of the forest, until she approached the stone edifice. *If you're wrong,* she thought, eyeing the circular staircase warily, once she had forced the door open, *you are going to get stuck, and no one will find you.* Fortunately, for the first time that day, luck was on her side. The inner doorway pushed open easier, and then she was on the roof, standing before him.

"The itinerary is nearly all daytime events," she told him, seating herself on his knee. "There's dinner and dancing every night, of course, but after that . . . Well, we're either supposed to retire to our beds like good little septons or else we're meant to be wanton, I suppose. It doesn't seem fair. Some of the couples played croquet together today. It's a beautiful lake for rowing; that's what I was supposed to do this afternoon. I went riding this morning with Lord Gorthund. He's a fine rider, and he seems very . . . well, he seems very orc-like. I heard more about horses than I ever cared to. He's pleasant enough, I suppose. If I had to marry him, I could make myself be happy, eventually, but he was not impressed with my riding skills, so I'm sure that's no longer an option. But then, after riding, my head ached, and I was so tired, so I went to sit under a tree to rest. I fell asleep, and I missed rowing. We had to be up so bloody early this morning for breakfast, and the sun hurts my eyes. I'm supposed to be back in the room getting ready for dinner right now because it's already that late, and I'm only just wandering back from my tree. How am I supposed to live in the daytime world, Silas? Things are so much prettier at night."

She wasn't sure when she had begun to cry, but it all seems so futile and hopeless. "I don't know what I'm supposed to do now. You ruined me, Silas. How am I supposed to go back to a life in the sun? How am I supposed to make myself be happy?" She shuddered when his fingertips brushed the loose tendrils of her hair away from her face, his whisper at her temple.

"It's alright, little moth. The moon is lovelier than the sun, and you deserve only lovely things." He had been hard and unyielding when she arrived on the rooftop, but now he was warm and alive beneath her, his lips hot against hers. Despite her anger and hurt, she did not pull away. She loved him, and denying it was pointless.

"Would you like to join me this evening after dinner, Miss Eastwick, to row on the lake?"

The sob that broke from her was embarrassingly noisy. His arms were steady around her, his scent warm and familiar, and at the horizon, the sun had disappeared.

"I would like that very much, Lord Stride."

Silas

When he was an adolescent, he and his brother had had a great row over whether or not he could go sailing for the night. The sea had been rough, and all evening long, great white caps had slammed into the base of the cliffs, inky black and angry. It was a dangerous sea, not one that anyone had any business traversing, not that night. But his brother was going out, and he couldn't understand why *he* could not go as well.

"It's too dangerous for you, and you can't even swim. Besides, you don't need to know how to sail on water like this. I do." Cadmus had always been the rational one. He favored their father, both in looks and temperament, while Silas and Maris looked like their mother. Silas had inherited her capriciousness as well, their father had been known to mutter.

"You can't tell me what to do. If I say I want to go out on the boat with you, I'm going to. There's no reason I can't do anything that you're able to —"

"Stop acting like a child, for once in your life!" His brother's voice was hard like steel, sharp and thunderous. "You're going to be the Marquis, Silas. You need to start acting like it. I get to go, because my life isn't worth anything. Yours is. You don't get to have it both ways, Silas. You don't get to have everything you want. So either grow up and start acting like a man and get the respect you deserve, or keep acting like a child forever and be treated like one."

It was a completely different situation, but he had the feeling his brother wouldn't see it that way. He was still acting like a child. Was still trying to have it both ways. He thought he could have everything he wanted, and in the process he had lost her, the only thing that mattered.

He had no idea what the building had been used for originally. Rounded walls on one side, buttresses on the other, and arched windows of winking clear glass. It did not appear to be a chapel, nor was it a military installation. Regardless, it was far enough from the main house to serve his purposes.

His heart was heavy when he'd ascended the roof at dawn. The sight of her dancing with the other monstrous men in attendance had been a lance to his heart, not as stony as he had originally thought it to be, but nothing could have prepared him for her words, for her bitter hurt and anger, and the worst part — her tears, and knowledge that he was the reason for them. She was going horseback riding that day, from the sound of it. Horseback riding and rowing and croquet and whatever other frivolous nonsense they did in the sunshine. Most importantly, Silas thought despondently, she would be doing it without him.

He thought about *that* night, how he *knew* what he'd felt, and instead of facing it like the lord he was supposed to be, he had run from it like the child he was, hurting her in the process. He no longer wanted to fake his own death and run off to play pirates with his brother. He wanted someone to actually push him from the roof. Let Maris have the title; she would do a better job with it anyhow. Let his marble body shatter and splinter, for he would never be good for anything ever again if he could not be good for her.

No. That was more than he deserved. That was still running away, still acting like a child, still leaving everyone else in his life to make accommodations for him, to pick up the pieces, and fix what he had broken. He needed to accept whatever decision she would make. He needed to go home and face his future, retire his rakish ways, and give his poor sister some peace, once and for all.

It was then that he heard it. He was barely cognizant of the fact that sound was coming back to him, that he had somehow already spent an entire day frozen in the sunlight. Her voice, heavy with melancholy and inexorably sad. He listened to her describe her disaster of a day, and her tears broke his heart anew. She was sweet and beautiful and kind, and deserved nothing but good things. Life had dealt her wretched hand, and any one of these monstrous lords would have been lucky to call her his . . . but she was sitting with him. Despite her anger, the hurt he'd caused her, despite her words, she had come back. *It's not too late.*

"Would you like to join me this evening after dinner, Miss Eastwick, to row on the lake?"

Now they were entering the ballroom once more, a shiver of déjà vu up his spine, and he was determined to right all that he had wronged. It couldn't be too late. He wouldn't let it be.

The first sight of her in her dress nearly made him stumble. It was an airy pink confection with what he could only describe as an indecently low neckline. Her every lovely asset was on display, but none was as beautiful as the smile she gave him as she approached. Her eyes were full of trepidation, but she wanted to believe him. *It's not too late.*

"Miss Eastwick, you're looking ravishing this evening. I was hoping I might ask you to join me outside for a moment. I would like to have a word with you, and I fear it cannot wait."

Her eyes flickered back, and he recognized the two young women he had seen her speaking with the previous evening. They were already paired off, he knew. One with his friend Casselon, and the other with Warwick. "Alright," she murmured hesitantly. "But we shouldn't be long; they'll be starting soon."

As soon as they were on the veranda, all of his practiced words left him. He was a fool, and he did not deserve her. "I don't deserve you, Eleanor." *Not the way you'd meant to start off, but you may as well be honest for a change.* Her eyes widened. "And I'll never deserve you. I think that's the most important part for you to know. You never have to feel as though you are earning anything with me because I will always be in your debt simply for having me. I'm not a good man, Miss Eastwick. I am jealous and lustful and childish and vain."

"You are all those things, yes."

"I am. There's no denying it. I am a liar and a rake, and a spoiled child. And I will never deserve to have a woman as fine as you at my side. But if you give me another chance, little moth, I will spend every night of the rest of my life showing you that I *can* be worthy of your heart. I will cherish you for the rest of my days. Come home with me, Eleanor. Be my wife, and let me spend the rest of my life showing you that I can be a man who deserves you."

Her eyes were full of tears, her lip caught between her teeth, but she said nothing. A little nod, raising a hand to wipe her eyes. He swooped forward with his handkerchief, pressing into her palm.

"Thank you. We — we should go back in. I don't want the Countess to think I've slept through the entire day's events."

His heart fell. She was moved, but not moved enough. That was what he thought, at least until they reentered the ballroom, the music already begun.

"Will you dance with me, Lord Stride?"

His heart was in his mouth as he took her hand. They entered another blasted quadrille, and he cursed the entire idiotic trend. Silas relished the weight of her hand in his as they moved through the steps, his hand at her waist, her hand at his shoulder. The music ended, and everyone applauded.

"Will you dance with me again, my Lord?"

She was looking up at him with her luminous eyes, and he knew that every word he had uttered was true. He would spend the rest of his miserable existence attempting to be someone who deserved her. *But that doesn't mean you need to start behaving like a bloody chaplain, not with her.*

"Why Miss Eastwick," he drawled into her ear, gratified at her smile, "I do believe you are sending the message to the rest of the guests that you have made a preference in your chosen suitor."

"I believe it does," she agreed nonchalantly. "One does hear such tales of butterflies and moths, you know, it seems rather silly to go risking it all now on a horse in a manure and mud-soaked field."

"It does indeed. Particularly as I've read that horses only know how to make love in one position. That sounds dreadfully dull to me." The music queued up. A waltz. *Perfect.* "What would you like to do after we row on the lake this evening, my dear?" They moved into the music, bodies flush, that lovely little lip trapped between her teeth again.

"I'd like for you to bring me home."

"That sounds perfect to me, little moth." He dipped her gracefully, his wings opening to shield them from the prying eyes of those behind them as he kissed her neck. "Miss Eastwick, this is a positively scandalous dress. Wherever did you get it?"

"I borrowed it from one of the other girls, actually. Uncle Efraim sent me beautiful dresses with necklines I knew you would think were far too high, and my neighbor's father altered all of her hers to look like this." Another turn, his hand slipping lower on her back, just over the swell of her delectable behind. "And besides, Lord Stride, don't you know?"

The music ended, applause, but she was pulling him down to her, to meet her lips.

"The scandal is the point."

My dearest Lord Ellingboe,

I can't thank you enough for contacting me last month regarding our shared vexation. You were absolutely right — a perfect match. It took a bit of maneuvering, but I managed to keep them on schedule.

The twenty percent of the bride's dowry I was promised for my assistance can be paid in silver. I will be putting the remainder into funds for the young ladies. I have every confidence that we will make good matches for them when the time comes, but as I'm sure you're aware, the burden on young women is great, and having their own financial freedom from their husbands will save them unhappy futures.

It was a pleasure doing business with you, Efraim. I'm thrilled we were able to reach a denouement that satisfied all parties, and I do hope we will see you at Basingstone for the wedding.
Yours affectionately,

Lady Maris Stride

Epilogue

The Moth and the Butterfly

The manor at Basingstone was an oasis of shaded walls, turned slate in the encroaching twilight, its hundred palladium windows flat and muted, reflecting the dusk sky. The roses smelled just as sweet as they did at noon, the topiaries cast long, leaping shapes across the walkway, and as she walked, the sound of a nightingale filled the air with its sweet song. The rolling hills around them were turning black as the sun turned his face away, and behind the house, the waves crashed in a uniform intensity, a non-stop push and pull against the rocks.

The moon temple was one of the most beautiful buildings she had ever seen. Stained glass windows in shades of blue and violet surrounded the entire cylindrical structure, and the story they told — of the moon goddess and the life cycle of a moth — had brought her to tears more than once. Because of its shape, the temple possessed the sort of acoustics that made every note echo and waver, and the lure of opening her throat and running through her repertoire standing in the middle of the circle was sometimes too great an enticement to deny. There were often one or two members of the pious sitting on the long benches giving thanks to the moon mother, and Eleanor did not want to be disrespectful, but the mothfolk who lived on the grounds had assured her repeatedly that it was an honor to have their temple serenaded by the Marchioness of Basingstone.

She was humming that evening as she followed the stone path. Past the grape arbor, past the gazebo, following the path around the lilacs to the doorway. She was still humming as she entered, not pausing her song as she dipped her head respectfully to the small group of mothwomen who were there, continuing on up the circular stone staircase. He would be waking up soon, and she would be there to greet him when he did.

Eleanor considered all that had transpired over the past four months as she seated herself on his knee. Her husband had been asked to stand at the wedding of his friend, the Duke of Warwick . . . who'd happened to be marrying her friend from the ball, Penelope Essex, who'd brought more books than ball gowns, and had still captured the heart of one of the most eligible bachelors in attendance.

"Do you know if you hadn't let me borrow that dress, I'd probably be a washerwoman right now? I know Silas too well. He's a fool for a daring décolletage."

Both women fell into a fit of laughter, and the bride wiped at her eyes.

"*Dramatic* is a ridiculous understatement. I can't believe my father thought I would —"

She waved the thought away, and Eleanor stood, patting her friend's beautiful copper hair beneath her headpiece.

"You look beautiful. I'm so happy for you, Penney."

"I'm happy for both of us. And just think — now we each have someone to talk to at those wretched parties."

Her own wedding was a rather staid affair, the pomp and pomposity that had been tentatively planned being upended when Lady Maris unexpectedly went into labour.

"It's honestly for the best," she panted when Eleanor had crouched at her side. "Any lord you might think to invite, his wife or daughter has likely already become intimately acquainted with my brother. Pushing him off the roof was a fine idea three months ago, but now we have need of him again, my dear."

Eleanor leaned forward to press her lips to his cold, marble mouth. She had a great need for her husband, as a matter of fact. A need that had been kindled when she rode atop him that morning, gripping the back of his throne for leverage as she rolled her hips, bouncing on his cock. She'd had need for him all day long, once she'd risen, sometime after noon. It was as if someone had lit a match just beneath her skin, and the flame had rippled out, igniting in her core. She burned for him, and there was only one way to extinguish the fire.

Dragging her nails down his marble chest, she scraped over his stomach, detouring around his groin to tease his well-muscled thighs. His cock was a rigid marble staff, jutting into the air as if it were waiting to have a flag run up it, just as swollen and stiff as it had been when she had left him that morning.

"Do you like the way my cock fills you, Lady Stride? Are you ready to come for me? I want to feel this sweet pussy flower squeeze me." His words had been a taunting growl at her ear, holding her steady as she rode him, one final bit of pleasure before he turned.

Silas liked emptying his balls just before dawn, claiming his sleep was most restful after a good fucking, and then again shortly after twilight, when he woke, clearing his head for the night to come. Most nights she loved obliging him, for Silas Stride was a rake of his word and always, always saw to her pleasure . . . but some nights it was good to remind him that even the Marquis of Basingstone could not always get everything he wanted.

She had become very good at learning how to time her climaxes. Eleanor wished she could say it was an accident, that she often came around her husband's cock just a moment before he turned, clenching him tightly with her muscles, milking him as she spasmed, her arm around his neck as she moaned out her pleasure . . . just too late for him to spill his seed.

It was an exquisite torture. He would be right there, poised on the edge of his peak, his knot swollen and throbbing, heavy bollocks pulled tight to his body, eager to empty, and then . . . nothing, as he stiffened to marble, unable to move, unable to cum, unable to voice his frustration at all. He would be left with the aching agony of unfulfillment all day until she returned at dusk to put him out of his misery, as she was readying to do then.

"I'm sure it wasn't too bad, darling," she murmured, kissing his jaw as she cupped his balls, squeezing the unyielding stone. It was just close enough to twilight that she knew he could feel her touch. She dragged her fingers up his cock slowly, rubbing her thumb over the pronounced ridges, before dropping to her knees. "You've been a very good boy lately; I think you've earned this." She licked a broad stripe up his swollen shaft, grinning at how fat and full he was. He was likely going to erupt the instant he regained movement, and she was going to be ready. In the meantime, she would give him a bit of encouragement.

Her lessons with the Marquis of Basingstone had not ceased after the ball. Her husband had been a world-class rake, after all, and it seemed foolish to stop improving her own love-making skills once they were wed. It was for her betterment and their shared enjoyment, and Eleanor found she did *so* enjoy taking him to pieces with her mouth. She laved her tongue over his cockhead, pressing into the seam of his slit, letting her teeth graze over the flared marble edge. She hummed again as she sucked him deeply, tightening her lips on her pullback and releasing him with a *pop*.

The sun had disappeared beyond the edge of the world, and she knew she only had a matter of minutes, if that. The first press of his cold marble tip made her gasp, as it always did, shivering as she sunk down on him slowly, the only thing that could soothe the fire in her blood. It had been a challenge, at first, learning to take him this way. The unyielding hardness coupled with his girth was an eye-watering press, and it had been painful until she'd learned that backing up on him was a gentler angle, easier for her muscles to loosen and her cunt to swallow him.

"It's so unfortunate that you were left in such a state, my lord," she murmured, twisting her head back to kiss the corner of his mouth. His face was frozen in a grimace, the agony of being past the point of no return and still unable to achieve completion, twisting his handsome features. She began to move, fucking herself on her husband's marble cock, every vein and ridge that she loved, frozen for her enjoyment. The ridges at the base of his head rubbed over the spot within her he had discovered, one that made her toes curl and thighs tremble, as they did then. "It makes it far too easy to take lewd advantage of you whilst you sleep. I wonder how quickly you're going to spill your seed when you wake."

It did not take long for her question to receive its answer. Eleanor cried out in surprise as she was pushed forward, his arm around her waist breaking her fall, somehow winding up on her hands and knees at the base of his throne, his cock hot and alive, driving into her savagely.

"Minx," he hissed at her neck. His feet were planted firmly on the ground, and it felt as if he were using his entire lower body to thrust into her. His thighs flexed, the slap of his balls an obscene percussion, and Eleanor keened. "You are going to pay for that, you devious little —" He dropped to his knees, covering her body with his as his cock erupted, words forgotten. Eleanor linked her fingers with his as he groaned against her shoulder, fangs nipping at her skin, wide wings stretching, covering them like a canopy. He had stayed his knot, and she felt it pulsing at the lips of her sex as he emptied, relieved he'd had the cognizance to understand she was not sufficiently prepped to take the protrusion. Incorrigible, but the very best butterfly. She stretched an arm back to stroke his ear as his cock spit up the final vestiges of his day-long torture, one final spurt before his hips eased their fervor.

When he finally slumped against her, pulling out carefully a moment later, she turned into his arms. "You know, it's very easy to take advantage of you when you sleep with your cock out."

"Minx," he repeated, wrinkling his nose. "I thought about trying to tip myself over this morning, thought I might be able to break it off, put an end to the agony."

"Well, it's a good thing you didn't. The Duchess of Sackwell has taken to giving me advice on how to balance my humours to best conceive a child, and it involves taking the oil of a fish and a weekly bloodletting. I don't want to know how they get oil from the fish, Silas."

"Tell the Duchess of Sackwell," he drawled, his tone a supercilious slide of satin, "to worry about her own bedroom. Ours is perfectly healthy, thank you very much. Actually, when she comes for your recital next week, I'll tell her myself."

"You'll do no such thing, you dreadful man."

The upcoming recital was both a cause of giddy excitement and crippling nerves, the first time she'd be singing publicly since she'd left Paris. An Evening of Music, hosted by the Marquis and his wife, had already been thoroughly investigated by the High Tea in two different columns, breaking down the short list of noblewomen — wives, sisters, and daughters — who would all be taking part, playing the harp, the piano, and singing. They'd made no mention of her past at all, as if she were a dead end, a dearth of information turning itself up, and it made her wonder if the infamous Lady Grey was someone they knew.

"Thank you for not knotting me," she added as an afterthought. "I wasn't ready for it."

"A skilled butterfly has no need to injure the flower, little moth," he sniffed, drawing her into his arms again once the banyan was tied snugly at his waist. "What would you like to do this evening?"

Eleanor sighed, pressing her nose against him. She had table coverings to pick out, and Kestin would likely already be lurking outside the lord of the manor's study, waiting with a list of grievances. There was much to do before her recital . . . but there was no end to what the two of them could do together once the sun went in. Everything, she thought, leaning up to kiss the corner of his wide, smirking mouth, was prettier in the dark.

For more of the Monsters Ball, go on to book two in the series, *the Monstrous Duke and I* by Dee St Holm

Confirmed wallflower Penelope Essex has every intention of tending her brother's library for the rest of her days. But first, she must survive the Monsters Ball.

Held at a remote gothic estate, the three-day ball is rife with monstrous nobles all determined to claim a mate. They'll do whatever it takes to seduce her into hidden corners, to tempt her into signing a marriage contract. Escaping with her spinsterhood intact seems impossible, until she spots her childhood crush: the now monstrous Duke of Roth.

Lord William Warwick is normally as cool as the cold fire covering his body. When he became a frost-flame demon, he swore he'd never take a mate. Yet when he sees Penny Essex struggling to resist three monstrous nobles, he rushes to her side and pretends to be her fiancé.

A fake betrothal is the perfect cover. Except the longer they're together, the more she wants his fire to claim her. But will her duke treasure her heart and her beloved books, or will their passion send them both up in flames?

Read it here: https://amzn.to/3Y8jKCs

THE *Monstera* BALL

To Ravish A Rogue

Coming Autumn 2023 – A Talons & Temptations Historical Monster Romance Novel

"**B**oy. You there, boy! Where did you come from? Did you think to be a stowaway? Are you too stupid to know you were meant to hide for that?"

Lirian turned, narrowing his eyes at Stride's sharply barked words. The new crew was being lined up on deck for introduction to the rest of the officers and to the captain, the smallest member being the object of his second-in-command's ire. It was the boy Lirian had watched coming up the gangplank before the sight of bronzed tits had swayed his attention, and his eyes narrowed again.

The young boy was not a boy at all; he could tell now that he was at a closer distance, although they had gone to lengths to suggest otherwise. Slight and thin, their baggy clothes did an admirable job of hiding any hint of their true form. The woolen stockings they wore were loose and bagged slightly, voluminous breeches ballooned around their knees, while a long linen tunic tented over narrow shoulders, coming to rest partway down their thighs. A cap covered their hair, the fringe of brown curls that had escaped giving them an unruly, unkempt air. It was impossible to tell what the oversized getup concealed. It could have been wings or another set of arms, or a pair of tits as lush and soft as the ones that had just been displayed for him. They were petite and scrawny, and while he couldn't immediately tell their gender or species, what he *could* discern was that they were not a preteen boy. Not a boy, and he suspected not a shifter. They lacked the otherworldly air of sea sprites and moved too clumsily to be a nymph. *But there is a glamour there.* A glamour a shifter would not possess. He could just barely see the outline of shimmer, a slight waver at the edges of their silhouette, so slight that he could nearly persuade himself he imagined it.

"M-me, sir?"

"No, the other lad I've never laid fucking eyes on."

The boy turned their head as if there might indeed be another youth beside them, and Lirian was obliged to stifle his laughter. *A girl.* As soon as the thought crossed his mind, he knew he was right, replaying in his mind the soft swish of their hips. *Not a girl. A woman. One who normally wears gowns and corsets, not breeches. One who has studied magic.* He'd heard stories of gods and shapeshifters able to change their form into whatever suited them, but the act of casting a glamour on one's appearance was not widely taught. If it were, he would have learned the blasted lesson years earlier. An apprenticeship with a crone was necessary, learning the old way and older magic, and the knowledge was traditionally only passed from mothers to daughters.

There was a woman on his ship, one who knew magic, who was playing at being a boy. Lirian didn't know why, but until he found out, he decided going along with the chit's deception was his wisest course.

"*Yes*, I fucking mean you," Stride snapped, the new-comer jumping to attention like a little soldier. "Where did you come from? What's your business here?"

"I—I signed up, sir. At the saloon two nights ago. Your men were there at a table, sir!"

Stride's eyes narrowed, his head turning sharply in the direction of the two crew members he had, indeed, left to man a table at the saloon while he went on to the tavern to do the same.

"What's your name then, boy?"

"Charlie, sir. I—I signed an X on the parchment, I did."

Stride blew out an aggrieved breath at the answer, and Lirian knew without needing to see the parchment in question that each man in the line had likely signed merely an X in place of their proper name. There were always more signatures than bodies that materialized. The crewmen in question had likely been well in their cups by the time they'd left to pursue their next diversion, and there would be no way to disprove the story. He was forced to admit, whoever she was, she'd done a bang-up job of constructing her alibi. *The imp!*

"And you've experience, have ya? At your age?"

"N-none, sir."

"Then what fucking good are you to me? Think this is a nursery, do ya? That we mind homeless whelps from every port?"

"Cabin boy, Mr. Stride," Lirian called out, surprising himself. "May I remind you, mine went missing?"

He watched as the boy — the *witch*! — turned at the sound of his voice. He wondered how long she had been watching his ship, watching his crew. She knew they had been recruiting in the saloon, knew to which ship they belonged, knew their leaving routine well enough that she had been here before dawn, her little disguise in place. She had planned long for this, he was willing to bet, but he could see in her eyes that she had not planned on him. She had been watching them clearly, knew their routine, had listened in on their conversations, but she had not seen hide nor hair of the ship's captain, for he had been tucked away in his cabin like a naughty child, and the fact that such a vital segment of her plan had escaped her knowledge clearly rankled the girl.

Lirian felt the drag of her eyes up his form, taking in his size, his grin, the ridges on his forehead that told the world what he was. Her face bore a look of consternation, and what a face it was. Beneath the mop of curls, she was fine and delicate. Wide eyes, a pert, upturned nose, a lush little rosebud of a mouth. Her cheeks had a rosy flush, her neck an elegant white column, the baggy shirt showing off an eminently kissable throat. How she thought she would pull off this deception, he had no idea. He did not know her plan, did not know her reason for being there, but she bore keeping a close eye on, a task he suspected he was going to enjoy.

"He'll make a fine cabin boy. I want his things moved into my quarters. As for the rest of you lot, we run a clean ship. Plunder is split equally amongst the crew, and you're crew as long as you're pulling your weight. If you become another anchor weighing us down, you'll be cast off as such. Follow your orders; keep these decks scrubbed. The inimitable Master Stride is your quartermaster, and his word is law. This is *not* a democracy. If Mr. Stride asks you to jump, your ass had better already be in the air before you think to ask how high. Don't let this pretty face of mine fool you into thinking I'll be easier to deal with. We'll be traveling off-realm, and that means all hands on deck at every moment. Do I make myself clear?"

Lirian turned away to the chorus of "aye, captain," trying to pick out the disguised wench's voice, finding no trace of her. He motioned to his mate to continue, pushing himself up the staircase to the bridge as Cadmus continued to bark orders. This was where Lirian was most comfortable, at the helm of his ship, taking her out where nothing but the open horizon waited. The wheel was an extension of his hands, always sure of her heading, never fearing the darker waters and the beasts that lurked there.

The new cabin boy was a witch. Of that, he was certain. Now that he had been made aware of it, he could almost feel the sizzle of her magic, the pressure of it pushing against him, making him want to tip himself over the starboard rail and drop into the sea, where he would be safe from her eyes. Turning, he sought the girl out with his own eyes, finding her easily, as she was still staring at him with an indiscernible look upon her face.

"My trunks will have already been brought to my cabin," he called down, instantly catching *the boy*'s attention.

"Sir?"

"If you think I'm going to shout, you're very much mistaken. Am I correct in assuming your legs work?" Cadmus shot him a malevolent look, as he was still addressing the men, to which Lirian replied with a beaming smile. "Shake a leg, Charlie, before you get me in real trouble."

She pulled from the ranks uncertainly before quickly hopping up the steps when it was clear she'd not be reprimanded for doing so.

"Right. My trunks. I expect them to be emptied this afternoon and then brought down for storage. I take my tea promptly at the end of the noontide watch and dinner at the start of first watch. I want my tub filled for bathing every third day—boiled sea water, with a pitcher of milk and soap of lye. Every morning, you are to retrieve the night reports and have them ready with my breakfast. You will take the crow's nest for two hours every morning once I've been served."

He paused at last, glancing down to the runt. She had flushed — most becomingly, he thought — at the mention of his bath, and the dull red had continued to creep over her face as Lirian had continued. *And now for the coup de grâce.*

"You've already been set up in the crew's quarters?"

"Yes, sir."

Her voice was little more than a whisper, hardly that of a strapping boy of ten or twelve, and he fought the urge to grin, knowing well that his teeth were gruesome to behold at this close vantage.

"Well, go and retrieve your things. Do it now, before they're dismissed, and be certain not to leave anything of importance behind."

"M-my things, Captain?"

"Your personal effects, dear boy! Sleeping roll, anything you brought with you. Step lively now. You can leave your hammock; there's no tacking for it. But do it quickly, or you'll spend your first night on board sleeping in the bilge. I don't care to have my crew whipped, but our bos'n finds it quite soothing."

He watched from the corner of his eye as she drew in a shuddering breath.

"If I'm not meant to sleep in the crew's quarters, Captain, sir," she began haltingly, "then where am I to sleep?"

Her voice was dulcet, and it, too, possessed a golden shimmer of otherworldliness, one she couldn't hide even if she tried her damndest. *Of which she was doing a piss-poor job.* He would need to keep her as secluded as possible in order to keep her safe, at least until he ascertained her motives. Port Perico was a speck behind them at that point, and ahead, the sun broke over the waves in a white-gold blaze, burning off the haze that clung to the water's surface.

"You'll be staying in the captain's quarters, boy. Where is it you think you're working? If there's one drawback to piracy, it's the unfortunate nature of those bilge rats and scallawags it attracts. I don't know what sort of scum we picked up at this last port, but there's bound to be a pederast amongst them. You'll be far safer behind the only locked door on board, I assure you."

"*Pirates?*"

"Well, of course, lad. Didn't you say you had signed up at the saloon? Talked with the crew?" He glanced down, giving her stricken look a winsome, closed-mouth smile. "Put your X on the parchment? Surely you knew what you were signing on for? Come now, you look half about to cry. I didn't realize the crew had recruited ladies for this leg of the journey."

She stiffened at his dig, and then he *did* grin, wide and terrible, unable to help himself.

"I should hope not," she gritted out stiffly. "Frightful bad luck to bring a woman on board. Isn't that what they say, *sir*?"

"Full cover, Mr. Stride," he called out, ignoring her for the moment. "Let's take her to sea."

"You heard the captain, you worthless bunch 'a sots. Full cover!"

The bos'n echoed the order, and Lirian watched the girl blanch as the full sails were dropped, an impressive unfurling of slate grey, the foremast bearing their insignia, the upper torso of a beautiful woman with the lower haunches of a serpent. Perhaps, he considered, it might be wiser to show his hand, to call her bluff, and let fate blow them to their futures. He had cargo to unload in Atlantis, and the coin that would be earned from that journey would fund the next, and that alone had been enough for him to look forward to. Now though, he found himself looking ahead to the journey, wondering when he would learn her secrets, if she would bare them to him willingly, and if there was anything else she would be willing to bare.

"You came to the right place for frightful bad luck, in that case, my dear. Welcome to the *Malediction*."

~

Coming Autumn 2023, part of the Bonkers Romance Kickstarter, launching March 2023

Also By
C.M. Nacosta

Cambric Creek – Where the neighbors are a little unconventional and the full moon affects more than just the night sky. Sexy werewolves, adorable mothmen, and randy minotaurs welcome you to settle in and make yourself at home! (Author's note: Regardless of the series, all the books set in Cambric Creek are interconnected with overlapping characters. They can be enjoyed as standalones, but you get the full scope of the community across each book!)

Welcome to Cambric Creek!

For a full list of titles, please visit https://linktr.ee/ Monster_Baitfor one-click shopping!

Morning Glory Milking Farm was just another quick tug machine operated facility, cash he didn't need in the bank for doing what he would have done for free anyway. At least, that's what he thought. He wasn't looking for love, but it managed to find him anyway and now he's determined to prove that you *can* teach an old bull new tricks. Fall in love all over again with Violet & Rourke's romance . . . from the other side of the milking table.

PRE-ORDER NOW: https://amzn.to/3KHKpDb

About the Author

C.M. Nascosta is a USA TODAY bestselling author of Monster Romance and a professional procrastinator from Cleveland, Ohio. She's always preferred beasts to boys, the macabre to the milquetoast, the unknown darkness in the shadows to the Chad next door. She lives in a crumbling old Victorian with a scaredy-cat dachshund, where she writes nontraditional romances featuring beastly boys with equal parts heart and heat, and is waiting for the Hallmark Channel to get with the program and start a paranormal lovers series. **For exclusive stories, signed paperbacks, bookish merch and more, visit:** https://linktr.ee/Monster_Bait

The best way to hear about all things Monster Bait before anyone else is to become a patron: http://patreon.com/monster_bait

The second best way to stay up-to-date on release news and extras is to follow me on Instagram: https://www.instagram.com/cmnascosta/

The best way to hear about things several days later when I get around to building an email is to join my newsletter: http://cmnascosta.com/